SEND FOR PAUL TEMPLE

A Stage Play

Of

Mystery and Thrills

Francis Durbridge

WILLIAMS & WHITING

Titles by Francis Durbridge published by Williams & Whiting

1   The Scarf – television serial
2   Paul Temple and the Curzon Case – radio serial
3   La Boutique – radio serial
4   The Broken Horseshoe – television serial
5   Three Plays for Radio Volume 1
6   Send for Paul Temple – radio serial
7   A Time of Day – television serial
8   Death Comes to The Hibiscus – stage play
    The Essential Heart – radio play
    (writing as Nicholas Vane)

Murder At The Weekend – the rediscovered newspaper serials
and short stories

Also published by Williams & Whiting:
Francis Durbridge : The Complete Guide
By Melvyn Barnes

Titles by Francis Durbridge to be published by Williams &
Whiting
A Case For Paul Temple
A Game of Murder
A Man Called Harry Brent
Bat Out of Hell
Breakaway – A Family Affair
Breakaway – The Local Affair
Melissa
Murder In The Media
My Friend Charles
Paul Temple and the Alex Affair
Paul Temple and the Canterbury Case (film script)
Paul Temple and the Conrad Case

Paul Temple and the Geneva Mystery
Paul Temple and the Gilbert Case
Paul Temple and the Gregory Affair
Paul Temple and the Jonathan Mystery
Paul Temple and the Lawrence Affair
Paul Temple and the Madison Mystery
Paul Temple and the Margo Mystery
Paul Temple and the Spencer Affair
Paul Temple and the Sullivan Mystery
Paul Temple and the Vandyke Affair
Paul Temple and Steve
Paul Temple Intervenes
Portrait of Alison
Step In The Dark
The Desperate People
The Doll
The Other Man
The Teckman Biography
The World of Tim Frazer
Three Plays for Radio Volume 2
Tim Frazer and the Salinger Affair
Tim Frazer and the Mellin Forrest Mystery
Twenty Minutes From Rome
Two Paul Temple Plays for Radio
Two Paul Temple Plays for Television

This book reproduces Francis Durbridge's original script together with the list of characters but the eventual staging might have edited Durbridge's script in respect of scenes, dialogue and character names.

INTRODUCTION

Francis Durbridge (1912-98) was a prolific writer of sketches, stories and plays for BBC radio from 1933. They were mostly light entertainments, including libretti for musical comedies, but a talent for crime fiction became evident in his early radio plays *Murder in the Midlands* (1934) and *Murder in the Embassy* (1937).

In 1938 Durbridge created the radio dream team of novelist/detective Paul Temple and his wife Steve. *Send for Paul Temple* was broadcast from 8 April to 27 May 1938 in eight twenty-five minute episodes, and listeners bombarded the BBC with over 7,000 requests for more. So Durbridge responded later the same year with *Paul Temple and the Front Page Men*, then from 1939 to 1968 wrote another twenty-six Paul Temple radio thrillers of which seven were new productions of earlier cases.

To complete the picture of Francis Durbridge's career – in 1952, while continuing to write for radio, he embarked on a sequence of BBC television serials (not featuring the Temples) that achieved huge viewing figures until 1980. Then from 1971 in the UK and even earlier for German audiences he wrote stage plays that are still produced by professional and amateur companies today, and it is his contribution to the theatrical stage that concerns us here.

Durbridge made his name in the theatre world with convoluted plots where nothing is what it seems – more like Frederick Knott than Agatha Christie. He achieved success with *Suddenly at Home* (a long run at London's Fortune Theatre from 30 September 1971 to 16 June 1973), followed by *The Gentle Hook, Murder with Love, House Guest, Deadly Nightcap, A Touch of Danger, The Small Hours, Sweet Revenge* and *Fatal Encounter*. But mentioned above is the fact that his theatrical career began earlier in Germany, because there is no doubt that *Murder with Love* was originally written, translated and staged in Germany in the early 1960s as evidenced by a newspaper report (*Dürener Zeitung*, 17 January 1962) that he was then working on his first stage play. This was premièred as *Wettlauf mit der Uhr* in 1964, and a few years later a new version was staged as *Ein Lückenloses Alibi*. In fact Durbridge's cash ledger, in an entry dated 16 February 1963, recorded the receipt of £617 for the rights of a play that even then he called *Murder with Love*.

So clearly Durbridge's first stage play was not *Suddenly at Home* in 1971, but neither was it *Wettlauf mit der Uhr* in 1964. Instead we must go back to his first Paul Temple radio serial, the success of which made it inevitable that Paul and Steve would transfer to the theatrical stage. And this was achieved when *Send for Paul Temple* was produced at the Alexandra Theatre Birmingham from 25 October to 6 November 1943, followed soon after by a short run in Wolverhampton.

According to a review in the *Birmingham Post* of 26 October 1943: "There are some strange goings-on this week at the Alexandra Theatre where Paul Temple, the detective who has made a reputation on the radio, is in session. To provide incident for this exciting sitting, it seems that the Newgate Calendar has been combed for material. A couple of kidnappings head the list and lead on to sterner stuff in the form of poisonings, shootings and dope dealing. Bodies fall out of lifts; screams rend the night; an innocent-looking gramophone spits forth bullets; and cyanide finds its way into harmless brandy flasks." The review credits "Robert Ginns's likeable Paul Temple, Vernon Fortescue and Denis Goacher as the men from Scotland Yard, Angela Wyndham-Lewis as the discreetly intelligent woman journalist indispensable to the modern detective and Andrew Buck as Dr. Brightman, the perverted practitioner indispensable to the modern crime."

The play was also favourably noted in the "Chit Chat" column of *The Stage* (4 November 1943): "Under the direction of George Owen, the Alexandra Repertory Company have made a creditable production. Robert Ginns in the name part displays a pleasing personality, and Angela Wyndham-Lewis makes the most of limited opportunities as the reporter-heroine."

Looking at this play's typescript, there are elements of the first radio serial *Send for Paul Temple*. For example there is the first meeting of Paul and Steve, following the murder of Steve's brother Superintendent Harvey who has been pursuing a criminal called Max Lorraine (alias the Knave of Diamonds in the first serial, but in the stage play he is the Front Page Man). Also taken from the first radio serial is the murder at Scotland Yard, the meetings and double-crossings of the criminal gang, and the conclusion when Paul and Steve decide to marry. But generally the plot follows that of the second radio serial *Paul Temple and the Front Page Men*, and all characters in this stage play (except Danny Muller) had featured in that second radio serial.

This was undeniably Francis Durbridge's first professionally-produced stage play, and there is no evidence of further performances until the discovery of this script after some seventy years led to a reading on 15 November 2015 at Middle Temple Hall in London in support of the charity The Kalisher Trust. Directed by Joe Harmston, a professional cast featured Stanley Tucci as Temple, Sophie Ward as Steve, Hugh Dennis as Brightman, Jason Watkins as Gerald Mitchell, Paul Herzberg as Sir Graham Forbes, Daniel Hill as Chief-Inspector Reid, Ray Fearon as Inspector Hunter, Mark Farelly as Sergeant Leopold, Cassie Raine as Ann Mitchell, Andrew Paul as J.P. Goldie, Sarah Berger as Diana Fresnay, Keith Myers as Chubby Wilson, Martin Fisher as Danny

Muller, Simon Cole as Jimmy Mills and Iain Christie as Pryce.

And this stage play lives on, as it has recently been translated into German by Georg Pagitz as *Paul Temple muss her!* although a German stage production has yet to be finalised.

Melvyn Barnes
Author of Francis Durbridge: The Complete Guide (Williams & Whiting 2018)

SEND F0R PAUL TEMPLE

A New Stage Play
Of
Mystery and Thrills
BY FRANCIS DURBRIDGE

CHARACTERS:
SIR GRAHAM FORBES
SERGEANT LEOPOLD
CHIEF-INSPECTOR REID
INSPECTOR HUNTER
DR BRIGHTMAN
GERALD MITCHELL
ANN MITCHELL
PAUL TEMPLE
PRYCE
STEVE TRENT
MR J.P. GOLDIE
CHUBBY WILSON
DIANA FRESNAY
JIMMY MILLS
DANNY MULLER
SWAN WILLIAMS
LUCKY GIBSON
SERGEANT DONOVAN

SCENES
There are three sets.
One full set and two in-sets

ACT ONE
Scene 1.   The office of Sir Graham Forbes, Assistant
            Commissioner of Police, Scotland Yard.

Scene 2.   The lounge of Paul Temple's flat ... The following
            afternoon.

ACT TWO
Scene 1.   The lounge of Paul Temple's flat.
            Continuation of the preceding scene.
Scene 2.   A warehouse near Redhouse Wharf.
            12.30 a.m., the same night.
Scene 3.   The lounge of Paul Temple's flat.
            3.30 p.m., the following afternoon.
Scene 4.   The office of Sir Graham Forbes, Assistant
            Commissioner of Police, Scotland Yard.
            Three hours later.

ACT THREE
Scene 1.   The office of Sir Graham Forbes, Assistant
            Commissioner of Police, Scotland Yard.
            Fifteen minutes later.
Scene 2.   A warehouse near Redhouse Wharf.
            9.15 p.m., the following evening.
Scene 3.   The lounge of Paul Temple's flat.
            Almost twenty-four hours later.

1

ACT ONE
SCENE ONE

The office of Sir Graham Forbes, Assistant Commissioner of Police, Scotland Yard.

It is a first-floor room looking towards the Thames Embankment. The windows are in the left wall.

There are several ledgers, files, etc, prominent on the walls together with a large plastic built-up map of the central London area. Sir Graham's desk and chair stand left of centre, a chair facing them. There is another desk further down stage complete with typewriter, dictograph, etc. The main door is back centre at right angles to the window. On the right wall and facing Sir Graham's desk is a second door leading to a private office.

When the curtain rises, SIR GRAHAM FORBES is stood by the side of his desk reading a copy of the Daily Telegraph. He is a man of about fifty-five, medium height, sharp features, and rather brusque. Suddenly, he places the newspaper on the desk and presses the button on the dictograph.

FORBES: (*Into dictograph*) Tell Inspector Hunter I want to see him! (*He switches the dictograph off*)
There is a knock on the main door and CHIEF INSPECTOR REID enters. He is a rather dour Scotsman.
REID: Sorry I'm late, Sir Graham. I was detained by Mr Mitchell.
FORBES: That's all right, Mac. I've only just arrived.
REID: Any news of Harvey, sir?

FORBES: Yes. (*After a moment*) Harvey's dead. He died just before six o'clock this morning.

REID: Good God, I never realised it was that serious!

FORBES: (*Softly*) No. No, neither did I.

REID: (*Suddenly*) Well, have you seen The Daily Express, sir?

FORBES: No, but I've seen The Telegraph! How in heaven's name did the press get hold of the Blakeley story?

REID: (*With a sigh*) I don't know. (*Ominously*) The Front Page Men are certainly on the front page now, Sir Graham – and things are going to look pretty nasty for us unless we get this Blakeley business straightened out.

FORBES: The Express didn't make any reference to the Granville affair?

REID: (*Surprised*) Why, no! What makes you mention the Granville affair, now?

FORBES: (*Softly*) I don't know, Mac. Ever since we've had this Blakeley case on our hands, I've found myself thinking of the Granville affair. I don't quite know why ... on the face of it there doesn't seem to be any connection.

REID: The Granville child was kidnapped months before we even heard of the Front Page Men. The book itself was only published in January.

FORBES: M'm ...

There is a tiny pause.

REID: (*Thoughtfully*) It's funny you should be talking about Lester Granville, I saw him the other night an' ...

FORBES: (*Surprised*) You saw him?

REID: Only on the pictures, Sir Graham. They're showing one of his old films at the Pavilion.

FORBES: (*Grimly*) I'd have given ten years of my life to have saved that child of his, Mac. She was the only thing he had left in the world after his wife died.

REID: (*Thoughtfully*) Aye, that was a nasty business an' no mistake.

There is a knock on the door and INSPECTOR HUNTER enters. He is a good-looking young man with rather a boyish personality.

HUNTER: You sent for me, sir?

FORBES: (*Pleasantly*) Yes, come in, Hunter!

SIR GRAHAM returns to his desk and opens one of the drawers.

HUNTER: (*Smiling*) Hello, Mac!

REID: (*Petulantly*) Hello!

FORBES: (*To REID*) I had a chat with Hunter last night. I thought it might be a good idea if he gave you a little help over this Blakeley affair.

REID: (*Peeved*) Certainly, if you think I'm needing help, Sir Graham.

HUNTER: (*Quietly, to FORBES*) How long have the Front Page Men been in existence, sir?

FORBES: Early in January, the novel 'The Front Page Men' was published and almost immediately it became a best seller both here and on the other side of the Atlantic. About the middle of February, the Margate Central Bank was raided and the head cashier – a young fellow named Sydney Debenham – was murdered. By the side of the body, we found this card.

SIR GRAHAM takes a small square piece of white cardboard from the drawer of his desk.

HUNTER: (*Taking the card and reading*) 'The Front Page Men' …

5

FORBES: The effect on the sales of the novel was of course phenomenal. About a fortnight after the Margate robbery, a smash-and-grab occurred in Bond Street. Two pedestrians who witnessed the robbery were murdered. Inside the window of the jewellers, we found another card – it was identically the same.

HUNTER: Sir Graham, I know it sounds rather stupid, but have you made any attempt to interview the author of the novel?

FORBES: (*Smiling*) The author of 'The Front Page Men' is apparently a woman who calls herself Andrea Fortune; but so far, at any rate, we've completely failed to locate her.

HUNTER: M'm. Who are the publishers?

FORBES: Mitchell and Bell, of Hanover Square. A young fellow named Gerald Mitchell is really the firm.

HUNTER: (*To REID*) Have you seen him, Mac?

REID: Aye, I saw him this morning. He's quite a pleasant young fellow, but he's never so much as set eyes on Andrea Fortune.

HUNTER: It seems to me a pretty big coincidence that Miss Fortune should wish to keep her identity a secret, especially in view of what's happened.

REID: Authors are a strange flock, Hunter, there's no accounting for certain of their peculiarities.

FORBES: Always excepting, of course, your learned friend Mr Temple!

REID: (*Irritated*) I can't understand it! At every conceivable opportunity, the newspapers refer to Paul Temple. They've even had placards out about the fellow – 'Send for Paul Temple'!! "Why doesn't Scotland Yard send for Paul Temple?" They're giving the general public a

6

completely warped impression of the man's importance.

FORBES: M'm – I wish it were only the general public, Mac. Even the Administration people have got a bee in their bonnet about the fellow.

HUNTER: It's a great pity the newspapers got hold of the Blakeley story.

FORBES: Yes, I'm rather worried about it. Sir Norman was warned not to get in touch with the police. That was the first message he received in fact, after the child disappeared.

HUNTER: You don't think they'll try any funny business, sir?

FORBES: (*Thoughtfully*) I don't know. I don't know, Hunter.

HUNTER: Did Blakeley have many visitors, Mac?

REID: (*Consulting a small diary which he takes from his waistcoat pocket*) No, very few. On the Tuesday, for instance, apart from tradespeople, a Dr Brightman called, and a Mr J. P. Goldie.

FORBES: J. P. Goldie? I don't remember Sir Norman saying anything about a Mr Goldie?

REID: He was the piano tuner, sir.

FORBES: Oh yes, of course.

REID: Goldie seems harmless enough. Used to be with Clapshaw and Thompsons in Regent Street. Started on his own about six years ago.

HUNTER: And Brightman?

SIR GRAHAM takes a folder from one of the drawers in his desk.

FORBES: M'm – we don't seem to know a great deal about Brightman. (*Consulting the folder*) According to Harvey's report; lives in Hampstead … Divorced his wife in 1929 …

HUNTER:	(*After a moment: to FORBES*) I was awfully sorry to hear about Harvey, sir.
FORBES:	Yes – a nasty business.
REID:	(*To HUNTER*) I suppose you know that Harvey was on his way to see Paul Temple when … the accident happened?
HUNTER:	Yes. (*After a pause*) Harvey was a friend of Temple's.
REID:	(*With a slow smile*) Are you a friend of Mr Temple's, Inspector?
HUNTER:	No, Mac – just an acquaintance.
REID:	M'm. (*After a moment*) Had Harvey any relations in town?
HUNTER:	I'm not sure. Richard was always rather reticent about his private affairs; although I do believe he had a sister in Cape Town.
REID:	Cape Town?
HUNTER:	Yes. Don't forget he was with the C.I.D. for nine years.
REID:	Oh, yes. Yes, I was forgetting that.

There is a knock on the door and SERGEANT LEOPOLD enters.

FORBES:	What is it, Sergeant?
LEOPOLD:	A Dr Brightman has called to see Inspector Reid, sir.
REID:	(*Surprised*) Brightman!
FORBES:	(*After a slight pause*) Wait a few minutes, then show him in here.
LEOPOLD:	Yes, sir.

Exit Leopold.

REID:	(*Thoughtfully*) Now what the devil does Brightman want?

FORBES: Apparently he wants to see you, Mac – but if you've no objections, I'd rather like to see Brightman myself.

REID: Go ahead, Sir Graham. Go ahead … (*To HUNTER*) Come along, laddie, we'll do a wee spot of eaves-dropping! (*Moves across towards the second office*)

FORBES: (*Moving the dictograph so that it partly faces the visitor's chair*) There's no necessity for that, Mac. (*He knocks down the switch*)

Exit REID and HUNTER.

There is a pause and then the door opens to admit SERGEANT LEOPOLD followed by DR BRIGHTMAN. BRIGHTMAN is a man of about fifty. Unlike most visitors to Scotland Yard, he is not in the least overawed by his surroundings.

LEOPOLD: (*Announcing*) Dr Brightman, sir.

Exit LEOPOLD.

FORBES: (*Pleasantly*) Good morning, sir.

BRIGHTMAN: (*Slowly advancing into the room*) I think there must be some mistake, I was under the impression that Chief Inspector Reid …

FORBES: I'm sorry but Chief Inspector Reid happens to be out of town at the moment. My name is Forbes – Assistant Commissioner.

BRIGHTMAN: (*Shaking hands*) Why yes, of course! How stupid of me! (*Smiling*) Oddly enough I actually came here with the hope of seeing you, Sir Graham.

FORBES: (*Smiles and indicates the chair facing the desk*) Sit down, doctor.

BRIGHTMAN seats himself, noting with a faint smile the position of the dictograph.

9

BRIGHTMAN: (*Taking off his gloves*) For a visitor to Scotland Yard, I find myself in a rather peculiar position, Sir Graham.

FORBES: Well, let's hope we can be of some service.

FORBES offers DR BRIGHTMAN a cigarette from the box on his desk but with a shake of the head BRIGHTMAN declines.

BRIGHTMAN: I'm rather afraid that's just the point. My purpose in visiting Scotland Yard is not to receive information, but rather to – er – impart it, as you might say.

FORBES: (*Smiling*) That isn't entirely unusual, Dr Brightman.

BRIGHTMAN: No? However: on Wednesday morning, the day after I had dined with Sir Norman Blakeley, your colleague, Chief Inspector Reid, paid me a visit. He was extremely polite, but for some reason or other I … er … inadvertently omitted to – er – …

FORBES: Why did you wish to see Inspector Reid this morning? Was it because you remembered something which might possibly be of some importance?

BRIGHTMAN: No. Not because I remembered something, Sir Graham, but because there is something of importance.

FORBES: (*After a slight pause*) What do you mean?

BRIGHTMAN: I mean that the Blakeley boy was not the first child to be kidnapped by The Front Page Men.

FORBES: Not … the … first … child? (*Puzzled*) I don't understand?

BRIGHTMAN: (*With a faint smile*) You must forgive me if I seem a little dramatic, Sir Graham, but my information is rather of a dramatic nature.

10

	(*Moves his chair nearer to the desk*) Two months ago, my own daughter was abducted by The Front Page Men, and I paid eight thousand pounds for her release.
FORBES:	(*Astounded*) You – you paid eight thousand pounds for …

BRIGHTMAN *slowly inclines his head. SIR GRAHAM is still rather nonplussed, but gradually recovers himself.*

FORBES:	When did this happen?
BRIGHTMAN:	During March of this year. The fourth to be precise.
FORBES:	But – but why didn't you consult the Yard about this matter?
BRIGHTMAN:	(*After a momentary hesitation*) To be perfectly honest, Sir Graham, because I didn't wish to take any risk.
FORBES:	It seems to me, my dear sir, that you took a very great risk.
BRIGHTMAN:	(*With a faint smile*) That, like so many things, Sir Graham, is a matter of opinion.
FORBES:	M'm. (*Suddenly*) Dr Brightman, when you delivered the ransom money did you cash a cheque?
BRIGHTMAN:	Naturally. I don't carry eight thousand pounds about with me in cash. I have an account at Lloyds in Manchester Street.
FORBES:	I see. (*Thoughtfully*) How did you receive the instructions – to deliver the money, I mean?
BRIGHTMAN:	At about ten-fifteen on the Monday morning, the telephone rang. Naturally, I answered it myself. It was a woman's voice. She sounded quite young, and rather pleasant. She said: "I am speaking for The

11

	Front Page Men. We want eight thousand pounds. The notes much not be numbered consecutively. Put the money in a brown leather suitcase and deposit it in the cloakroom at the Regal Palace Hotel. The case must be there by twelve-thirty tomorrow morning" …
FORBES:	(*Deeply interested*) Go on …
BRIGHTMAN:	The following morning I carried out the instructions. When I arrived home, Margaret, my daughter, was already waiting for me.
FORBES:	Was she all right?
BRIGHTMAN:	(*Nodding*) Perfectly.

The telephone rings and FORBES takes the receiver.

FORBES:	Excuse me. (*On the phone*) Hallo? … Yes, Turner? … (*Surprised*) What's that? … Yes, of course I'll see him! … No, don't do that. Ask him to wait in Superintendent Bradley's office … Yes … Yes, all right! (*He replaces the receiver; somewhat deep in thought he rises from the desk*) Dr Brightman, did anyone visit your house at all the day before your daughter disappeared? (*He presses a button on the desk*) I mean, any friends, business acquaintances, or …
BRIGHTMAN:	(*Thoughtfully*) No, I don't think so.
FORBES:	You're sure of that?
BRIGHTMAN:	Why, yes … I … (*Suddenly*) Just a minute! There was someone – an old fellow who calls about every four months to tune the piano. Oh, but he couldn't possibly …

SIR GRAHAM comes from behind his desk. He is obviously rather surprised.

FORBES:	A piano tuner!
BRIGHTMAN:	(*Faintly amused at SIR GRAHAM's astonishment*) Yes … a … piano … tuner …
FORBES:	(*Eagerly*) Do you remember his name?
BRIGHTMAN:	No, I'm afraid I don't. My butler did mention it, but …
FORBES:	(*Quietly*) Was it Goldie? J. P. Goldie?
BRIGHTMAN:	(*Rising, no longer amused*) Why … Why, yes – I believe it was! (*Suddenly*) Oh, but he couldn't possibly have anything to do with this business!
FORBES:	(*Smiling*) That, like so many things, Dr Brightman, is a matter of opinion.

There is a knock on the door and SERGEANT LEOPOLD enters.

LEOPOLD:	You rang, sir?
FORBES:	Yes, Dr Brightman is leaving, Sergeant. Take him through Kirkby's office, it'll be much quicker.
LEOPOLD:	Yes, sir.
FORBES:	(*Shaking hands with BRIGHTMAN*) Well, goodbye sir, and many thanks for calling.
BRIGHTMAN:	(*Rather surprised by the abrupt dismissal*) Good day, Sir Graham. If I can be of any further service, don't hesitate to give me a ring.
FORBES:	We shan't.

Exit BRIGHTMAN and SERGEANT LEOPOLD.

SIR GRAHAM returns to his desk and lifts the telephone receiver, as he does so he knocks the switch down on the dictograph.

REID and HUNTER enter from the outer office.

FORBES:	(*On the phone*) Tell Sir Norman I shall be down in about three minutes, Turner. (*He

13

	replaces the receiver) Well, what did you think of the loquacious Dr Brightman?
HUNTER:	He certainly lived up to his promise, I'll say that for him. Told his story very well, I thought.
REID:	Aye, quite the bedside manner.
HUNTER:	Was that Blakeley on the …
FORBES:	Yes. He called while Brightman was here. I gather it's pretty urgent.
HUNTER:	(*Anxiously*) I wonder if he's heard anything?
FORBES:	(*Thoughtfully*) I don't know.
REID:	Perhaps the poor devil's annoyed about the newspapers.
FORBES:	I should think that's more than likely. I'll see you both later!

SIR GRAHAM goes out.

REID crosses over to the small desk and opens one of the drawers.

HUNTER:	(*Rather puzzled*) Mac, did you believe that story of Brightman's?
REID:	Believe it? Why shouldn't I believe it? It was a grand story, full of interesting detail. (*He takes a small tin box from the desk and closes the drawer*)
HUNTER:	(*Earnestly*) Yes, but did you believe it?
REID:	(*Opening the tin*) The trouble with me is, I hardly believe anything these days. Simply no faith in human nature. It's a very distressing condition to be in, I can assure you. (*Offering HUNTER the tin*) Will you have a toffee?
HUNTER:	(*Smiling*) No thanks, Mac.

REID changes the position of the chair and makes himself comfortable at the desk.

14

REID: (*Faintly amused, and a shade supercilious*) Hunter, you're a bewilderment, young man. You can't quite make up your mind whether to believe Brightman's story or not.

HUNTER: (*Rather irritated*) I don't believe it. But I must confess I can't see his point in coming to Scotland Yard.

REID: Can't you? That rather surprises me now. I thought all you young fellows made a special study of the psychological aspect of a case.

HUNTER: (*A flicker of annoyance crossing his features and suddenly breaking into a disarming smile*) You've been reading too many detective novels, Mac, that's your trouble.

Suddenly, the centre door is thrown open and SIR GRAHAM FORBES re-enters. His face is tense, and he is obviously excited. He crosses to the telephone on the small desk.

FORBES: (*Into the phone*) Watkins? Sir Graham here ... Listen! ... I want to see Morgan ... Rogers ... Thornton ... Deal and Weston ... Yes, in my office – straight away ... (*He replaces the receiver*)

REID: (*Tensely*) What's happened?

FORBES: (*Turning*) Sir Norman's had a message! They want nine thousand pounds – and they want it by four o'clock tomorrow afternoon!

HUNTER: (*Astonished*) Nine thousand!

FORBES: (*Nodding*) Yes, and they want the money deposited in the telephone box at the corner of Eastwood Avenue.

HUNTER: (*Thoughtfully*) Eastwood Avenue?

FORBES: (*Crossing to the map on the wall*) This is a map of the central London area. I want you both to have a good look at it. (*HUNTER and REID cross over to the far wall*) There's the telephone box opposite that block of flats! (*He points to the map*) Now tomorrow, Mac, I want six of your men at the corner of Lenton Park Road, you see the point I mean?

REID: Aye, sir.

FORBES: (*Briskly*) Hunter, you watch the opposite end furthest away from the telephone booth. Have all the men placed ... and ready ... by three o'clock.

HUNTER: Yes, sir.

FORBES: (*Peering closer at the map*) The telephone box is here, opposite the block of flats and Eastwood Avenue. Now, if Weston and Deal park their car so that ... (*Suddenly pointing to a point on the map*) By the way, this flat would have a pretty good view of the box, wouldn't it?

HUNTER: It would from the side window, sir.

FORBES: (*Thoughtfully*) M'm. (*Suddenly*) Ring the janitor, Hunter, and find out who occupies it. (*Smiling*) I have a feeling that I should rather like to have tea there tomorrow afternoon. (*Peering at the map*) The address is ... 49, Eastwood Mansions.

HUNTER: (*Astonished*) 49, Eastwood Mansions!

FORBES: (*Puzzled*) Yes.

REID: (*Irritated*) What the devil is it?

HUNTER: Why – why that's Paul Temple's flat, sir! (*He looks across at REID and smiles*)

BLACKOUT

ACT ONE

SCENE TWO

The lounge of Paul Temple's flat in Mayfair. The following afternoon.

It is a very large flat and the lounge is pleasantly and comfortably furnished. The back wall is almost entirely covered by a very large panel bookcase, part of which swings away from the wall revealing the entrance to a concealed lift. To the extreme right of the bookcase opens out into a recess which contains a small radio-gramophone and an armchair. The large bay window stands almost at right angles to the recess, and on the same level. There is a modern cocktail cabinet down centre. Almost opposite the window, and on the extreme left of the bookcase is an alcove which leads to a hallway and the rest of the flat.

AT RISE: *GERALD MITCHELL is finishing a nervous cigarette. He is any age between forty and fifty. Tall, dark, and well dressed. No one is in the least surprised to learn that he is one of the very few successful independent publishers.*

ANN MITCHELL is seated on the settee, facing her husband with an amused air of tolerance discreetly mingled with feminine impatience.

ANN: Do come and sit down, Gerald!
GERALD: (*Irritated*) Oh, leave me alone! I feel irritable, Ann. I've been feeling like it all day! (*Stubbing his cigarette in the ashtray*) That damned detective certainly didn't improve matters!

ANN: (*Laughing*) Darling, I think I shall have to have you psycho-analysed! The way you're carrying on just because some dreary old detective asked you a lot of stupid questions!

GERALD: (*Irritated*) He wasn't dreary, and he didn't ask a lot of stupid questions. (*Thoughtfully*) I suppose he was quite charming really.

ANN: Then what's all the fuss about? After all, Gerald, you did publish the book, so the police were bound to have a word with you sooner or later.

GERALD: Yes. Yes, that's what Paul said. (*Anxiously*) He didn't seem to think there was any need for me to worry, did he?

ANN: Of course he didn't. And there isn't any need for you to worry, my sweet!

Suddenly, part of the panel bookcase swings open, revealing the illuminated interior of a lift. PAUL TEMPLE emerges, and the panelling returns to its original position. PAUL TEMPLE is a man of about forty. He is not what one would call handsome in the accepted sense of the word, but he has managed to combine the susceptibilities of the popular novelist with the charm and grace of a man of the world. At the moment he is carrying a book.

TEMPLE: You're still looking very gay, Gerald! What's the matter, Ann, haven't we convinced him he's not going to be shot at dawn? (*He crosses centre*)

ANN: (*Laughing*) I'm afraid not. The poor darling is still in the depths of despair.

TEMPLE: Well, here's the first edition I told you about. You'll find the Galsworthy story on page six.

GERALD: (*Taking the book*) Thanks. (*He hesitates*) Paul, you don't think there <u>is</u> any need for me to worry about this business?

18

TEMPLE: Of course not! If you hadn't published 'The Front Page Men' somebody else would have done so.

ANN: That's exactly what I've been telling him all along! Isn't it, darling? (*Pulling on her gloves*) We're supposed to be dining at The Savoy – which means I shall have to change. Then Gerald's dashing out to Denham.

GERALD: I'm going out there to have a chat with Cyril Heston. I don't know whether you've met him or not?

TEMPLE: (*Smiling*) Once. Does he still use Chanel?

GERALD: (*Faintly amused*) I shouldn't be in the least surprised! (*A shade brighter*) When do you think your new novel will be ready? We should like it in hand while the newspapers are running their 'Send For Paul Temple' campaign. You've no idea how it's affecting your other novels.

TEMPLE: (*Laughing*) I can guess.

ANN: Have the reporters been rather a nuisance, Paul?

TEMPLE: At times. (*Smiling, and with a nod towards the bookcase*) That's one of the advantages of having the lift. There's an entrance into Milford Street.

GERALD: (*Interested*) Is there really? I say, that is useful! (*Crossing towards the bookcase*) You know, I once saw a play at the Lyceum with a lift just like this.

TEMPLE: (*Laughing*) I'd like to bet a fiver they found a body in it?

GERALD: Rather! Second act curtain. Great goings on at the Baronial Hall!

ANN: (*Rather irritated*) Paul, what actually started The Evening Post on their 'Send For Paul Temple' campaign?

19

TEMPLE: About two years ago, I assisted Scotland Yard in the investigation of a crime known as the Tenworthy Affair.

GERALD: (*Thoughtfully*) I remember the Tenworthy Affair. You made several extraordinary discoveries which the police had completely overlooked. (*To TEMPLE*) Why, I do believe the police arrested a fellow called Wilson who had nothing whatever to do with the case? (*He crosses over towards the chair near the window for his hat and stick*)

TEMPLE: (*Thoughtfully*) Yes, Chubby Wilson.

ANN: (*Laughing*) Well, no wonder all the newspapers are …

ANN stops laughing and stares at GERALD with astonishment. He is stood by the window, staring down into the street below, his face a picture of surprise and fear. He turns.

GERALD: (*Excitedly*) I told you, didn't I? I told you there was something funny going on!

ANN: (*Alarmed*) Gerald … what it is?

GERALD: (*Returning centre*) I knew damn well they'd got their eye on me! You wouldn't believe it! You thought I was imagining things, didn't you? You thought I was being silly and … (*He notices that TEMPLE is now by the window*) Well … do you see him?

TEMPLE: (*Smiling*) Yes. Yes, I see him.

ANN: (*Alarmed*) Paul … who is it?

TEMPLE: It's all right, Ann, there's nothing to get worried about. It's only the detective who questioned Gerald about Andrea Fortune.

ANN: (*Puzzled*) But … I don't understand? What's he doing here?

20

GERALD: It's quite obvious what he's doing. He's trailing me!

TEMPLE: (*Amused, turning away from the window*) I don't think so, Gerald. Even if Scotland Yard wanted to put a man on your trail, I hardly think they'd use Chief Inspector Charles Cavendish Mackenzie Reid. (*Lapsing into a Scottish accent*) He's a verra' important man is Chief Inspector Reid ... 'Verra important! (*He glances towards the window again, and is obviously amused and interested*)

ANN: (*Suddenly*) Gerald, it's getting late. We'd better be going.

GERALD: (*After a slight pause*) Yes. Yes, all right.

TEMPLE: (*Returning centre*) I'd rather like you to stay for tea but ... (*Smiling at GERALD*) I've got Sir Graham Forbes calling at three-thirty.

GERALD: (*Astounded*) Sir Graham Forbes? You mean the Assistant Commissioner?

TEMPLE: Yes.

GERALD: (*Alarmed*) Paul ... forgive me ... but why is Sir Graham coming here? Is it because ...

ANN: (*Annoyed*) Gerald, please!

TEMPLE: (*Rather amused, shaking his head*) He doesn't even know I'm a friend of yours.

ANN: Of course not!

Enter PRYCE, a middle-aged manservant.

PRYCE: Sir Graham Forbes has arrived, sir.

TEMPLE: In a few moments, Pryce.

Exit PRYCE.

TEMPLE crosses to the bookcase, presses a concealed button, and the panel swings open.

TEMPLE: Where did you park the car?

ANN: I told Bentley to wait in Milford Street.

TEMPLE: Splendid!

TEMPLE waits for ANN and GERALD to enter the lift then follows. The panel closes.

PRYCE re-enters followed by SIR GRAHAM.

PRYCE: Mr Temple won't be long, sir.

FORBES: Thank you.

Exit PRYCE.

SIR GRAHAM glances round the room then very quickly passes over to the window. He stands for a short while staring into the street. Eventually he returns centre. He notes with interest the contents of the room and strolls over to the bookcase. He takes a book from the case and idly turns the pages. Suddenly, he replaces the book and picks up a small lace handkerchief from the floor near the bookcase. He is examining the handkerchief when the panel suddenly opens, and TEMPLE enters.

TEMPLE: (*Pleasantly*) Hello, Sir Graham! I'm sorry to have kept you waiting.

FORBES: (*Smiling*) You should tell your lady friends to be a little more discreet, Temple. (*He holds out the handkerchief*)

TEMPLE: M'm? Oh, thanks. (*He takes the handkerchief and throws it on to the small table*) Mrs Mitchell must have dropped it …

Pause.

FORBES: (*Crossing centre*) Nice place you've got here. Pretty handy for the West End, I should imagine.

TEMPLE: (*Smiling*) Very. And such a delightful view. On a clear day we can practically see the whole of Scotland Yard.

FORBES: (*After a slight pause*) So you've noticed them?

TEMPLE: (*Nodding*) Is that why you came here?

FORBES: M'm – m'm … I wanted to be able to keep an eye on things and picked on this flat as a likely spot.

(*Laughing*) I got something of a shock when I discovered it was yours.

TEMPLE: (*Quietly*) Why are they watching the telephone booth?

FORBES: Is it so obvious?

TEMPLE: No, I don't think so. (*Smiling*) … But I recognised Reid. (*He offers SIR GRAHAM a cigarette*)

There is a pause.

SIR GRAHAM lights his cigarette.

FORBES: You've heard of Sir Norman Blakeley?

TEMPLE: You mean the motor-magnate? Why yes, of course!

FORBES: Blakeley has a child. A boy … and three days ago he disappeared.

TEMPLE: (*Smiling*) Yes. It's in the papers.

FORBES: (*Ominously*) Yes, Mr Temple – it's in the papers. (*After a slight pause*) Blakeley received a note warning him not to get in touch with the police. It was signed – 'The Front Page Men.' This was on Tuesday, two hours after the child disappeared. (*TEMPLE nods*) At ten-fifteen yesterday morning, he received a telephone call. It was a girl speaking. She told him they wanted nine thousand pounds and the notes must be deposited in the telephone booth at the corner of Eastwood Avenue at four o'clock today … prompt …

TEMPLE: (*Quietly*) And he's going to deposit the notes?

FORBES: (*Nodding*) Yes, he's going to deposit them.

TEMPLE: Did Blakeley receive any visitors the day the child disappeared?

FORBES: Two. A friend of his named Dr Brightman, and an old chap named Goldie who calls two or three times a year to tune the piano.

TEMPLE: You've checked up on them?

FORBES: Yes. They seem pretty well O.K., so far as we can make out. (*Quietly*) Although, I'm just a shade doubtful about the piano tuner.

TEMPLE: Why do you say that? (*A slight pause*)

FORBES: Because by a strange, and rather remarkable coincidence, Dr Brightman had his daughter kidnapped about six months ago. He paid the ransom money, and the child was returned. The circumstances were almost identical with the Blakeley case – except of course for the fact that Brightman didn't consult the Yard.

TEMPLE: M'm – I take it that when you say the cases were identical, you mean that Brightman also received a telephone message, and that …

FORBES: I mean that, by a strange coincidence, on the day the Brightman child disappeared the piano tuner happened to be in the house.

TEMPLE: (*Slightly surprised*) You mean … Goldie?

FORBES: (Nodding) M'm – m'm … Mr J. P. Goldie. (*He looks at his watch*) I suppose you've read about Harvey?

TEMPLE: Yes.

FORBES: You knew that he was on his way here … when the accident occurred?

TEMPLE: Why, of course! He telephoned me.

SIR GRAHAM nods and turns towards the window. Before he reaches the window PRYCE enters, followed by CHIEF INSPECTOR REID.

PRYCE: Chief Inspector Reid has called to see Sir Graham, sir.

REID with a brief nod to TEMPLE hurries forward.

PRYCE goes out.

FORBES: (*Turning, obviously surprised*) Hello, Mac!

24

REID: (*Excited*) I'm sorry bursting in like this, Sir
           Graham, but … (*He hesitates*)
FORBES: (*Impatiently*) Well, what is it?
REID: It's Blakeley, sir.
FORBES: (*Urgently*) What about Blakeley?
A slight pause.
REID: He's … dead.
FORBES: Dead!
*REID nods, obviously a little relieved now that he has finally
broken the news.*
TEMPLE: (*Briskly*) Where is he?
REID: He's in the telephone box downstairs, sir. We've
           been watching it for almost two hours and the
           poor devil was on the floor all the time.
TEMPLE: But supposing someone had wanted to
           telephone?
REID: There was a small sign on the outside which said
           – 'Out of Order'. It was there when we arrived,
           sir.
FORBES: Who found Blakeley?
REID: (*Reluctantly*) Hunter did, sir.
FORBES: Was the suitcase there?
REID: (*Taking a small gilt-edged postcard from his
           pocket*) No. But there was this card on the ledge,
           sir – near the telephone.
FORBES: (*Taking the card and reading*) "Unlike Dr
           Brightman – he talked. The Front Page Men."
           (*Decisively*) Come along, Mac! (*To TEMPLE*) I
           may see you later, Temple. (*As TEMPLE crosses
           towards the alcove*) No, don't bother to come
           down – we can find the way!
Exit SIR GRAHAM and REID.
*TEMPLE rings for PRYCE then turns towards the window.
He stands for a little while obviously interested and is a shade*

25

*amused by the drama that is being enacted in the street below.
After a slight hesitation he returns centre, stands by the
telephone on the small table, and finally consults a diary
which he takes from his pocket. He finds the number he
requires but is still obviously undecided about using the
telephone. Suddenly, he replaces the diary, lifts the receiver
and dials. It is quite a little while before the call is answered.*

TEMPLE: (*On the phone, amused*) Hello? … Is that you,
Chubby? … (*Laughing*) You sound very cheerful,
I must say! (*A slight pause*) No … no, I just want
to see you … No, nothing like that … Just a
friendly chat … I said 'friendly', Chubby … M'm?
Well, there's no immediate hurry … (*Glancing at
his watch*) All right, if that suits you best … Yes
… Yes, of course … Goodbye. (*He replaces the
receiver*)

PRYCE enters.

PRYCE: Did you ring, sir?

TEMPLE: (*Casually picking up the lace handkerchief from
the small table*) Yes, I'm expecting Chubby
Wilson, Pryce. Don't treat him with quite such
dignified indifference this time.

PRYCE: Yes, sir. I'm very sorry about the last occasion,
sir.

TEMPLE: (*Laughing*) That's all right. (*For the first time he
examines the handkerchief, and his expression
changes. He glances towards the lift*) Pryce …

PRYCE: (*Turning*) Yes, sir?

TEMPLE: Did anyone call this morning while I was out?

PRYCE: Several reporters, sir.

TEMPLE: (*Thoughtfully*) No one else?

PRYCE: No, sir.

TEMPLE: You didn't invite any of the reporters into the flat
by any chance?

26

PRYCE: (*Surprised*) Why no, sir!

TEMPLE: (*After a tiny pause, turning the handkerchief over in his hand*) I wondered – that's all.

PRYCE: (*Smiling to himself*) There was one reporter who seemed very insistent, sir. She simply wouldn't take "No" for an answer.

TEMPLE: (*Slightly amused*) Wouldn't she, Pryce?

PRYCE: A very pretty girl too, sir. If – er – I may say so?

TEMPLE: By all means say so, Pryce. A very pretty girl who wouldn't take "No" for an answer! M'm! M'm! Sounds interesting.

PRYCE: I do wish I could remember her name, sir. I made particular note of it at the time, because I thought it sounded rather silly for a young lady.

TEMPLE: (*Indicating the initials on the handkerchief*) Does this convey anything to you?

PRYCE: (*Reading*) "S … T …" No sir, I'm afraid it doesn't unless … (*Suddenly*) Yes, that's right. That's right, sir! … Trent was the name … Steve Trent!!!

TEMPLE: Well, I'm inclined to agree with you, Pryce. Miss Trent certainly seems to have been a persistent young lady.

PRYCE: (*Bewildered*) I don't understand, sir? If the handkerchief belongs to …

TEMPLE: (*Interrupting PRYCE*) Sir Graham found the handkerchief and I naturally thought that Mrs Mitchell must have dropped it because … (*Thoughtfully*) … it was near the lift. (*Looking at PRYCE*) You don't suppose your enterprising young friend knew all about the lift by any chance, and decided to …

Instinctively, and with a sudden dart of suspicion, TEMPLE glances round the room. His eyes rest on the armchair in the recess. There is a pause, then in a flash he is across the room,

27

and taking a firm hold on the back of the chair he swings it round with a dramatic flourish.

STEVE TRENT emerges from the chair, in which she has been sitting with her back to the audience. She is very young, smartly dressed, and just at the moment rather apprehensive.

STEVE: (*Adopting a matter of fact manner*) Hello!

PRYCE: (*Turning towards TEMPLE completely nonplussed by STEVE's appearance*) This is the – er – young lady I was telling you about, sir.

TEMPLE: (*Slightly amused*) Yes, so I gathered. (*Dismissing PRYCE*) It's all right, Pryce.

PRYCE: (*Still staring at STEVE in bewilderment*) Thank you, sir.

Exit PRYCE.

STEVE: (*To TEMPLE*) He's rather sweet, isn't he? Quite the imperturbable butler. Except of course that he isn't imperturbable.

TEMPLE: (*Frowning*) I think perhaps I ought to warn you, Miss Trent, that I don't care for reporters.

STEVE: Then we have something in common, Mr Temple. I don't care for them either.

TEMPLE: (*After a tiny pause*) How long have you been here?

STEVE: Oh, about an hour. (*A slight pause*) Mr Temple, why do you think I insisted on seeing you …?

TEMPLE: Well, I rather imagine that you hope to get some sort of an exclusive interview.

STEVE: "Paul Temple's opinion of The Front Page Men?" "What Paul Temple thinks of Scotland Yard" …? (*Shaking her head*) That's not why I came to see you …

TEMPLE: (*Obviously interested*) What was your reason …?

A long pause.

STEVE: (*Looking at TEMPLE with almost intense interest*) Do you think Superintendent Harvey was murdered?

TEMPLE: (*Amused*) My dear Miss Trent, I don't see that it makes a great deal of difference what I think!

STEVE: (*Suddenly, with unexpected emotion*) Please! Please, answer my question! Do you think Superintendent Harvey was … murdered?

A tiny pause.

TEMPLE: (*Surprised by her attitude*) By Timothy, you are a remarkable young woman! First of all, you insult my …

STEVE: (*Interrupting TEMPLE*) You haven't answered my question!

Pause.

TEMPLE: (*Quietly*) Yes. Yes … I think he was murdered.

STEVE: (*Gently, speaking to herself*) I knew it! I knew it! I knew they'd get him … (*She turns towards the alcove*)

TEMPLE: (*Suddenly taking STEVE by the shoulders*) Why did you wish to see me?

STEVE: (*After a slight hesitation, looking up at TEMPLE*) Because I need your help. Because I need your help more than I've ever needed anything in my life before.

TEMPLE: It was Harvey who told you about the lift, wasn't it?

STEVE: Yes.

TEMPLE: Was he a great friend of yours?

STEVE: (*Gently*) Richard Harvey … was my brother.

TEMPLE: (*Surprised*) Your … brother?

STEVE: My real name is Harvey, Louise Harvey. I chose the name of Steve Trent for professional reasons.

TEMPLE: (*Puzzled*) When I suggested that your brother might have been murdered, you said: "I knew it! I knew it! I knew they'd get him!" What did you mean by ... "I knew they'd get him"?

STEVE: (*After a slight pause*) Why do you think my brother was coming to see you the night he was murdered?

TEMPLE: (*Thoughtfully*) I don't know. I'm not at all certain that he had any particular reason.

STEVE: He had ... a very good reason.

TEMPLE: Well?

STEVE: Richard was working with Chief Inspector Reid on the Blakeley case, and I'm almost certain that he had a theory which he wanted to discuss with you.

TEMPLE: A theory ...?

STEVE: About eight years ago, Richard was attached to what was then called Service B.Y. It was a special branch of the Cape Town Constabulary.

TEMPLE nods.

STEVE: At this particular time, a notorious gang of criminals were carrying out a series of raids on various jewellers within an area known as the Cape-Town Simonstown area. After months of investigation, Richard discovered that the leader of the organisation was a man who called himself Max Lorraine.

TEMPLE: Yes. I've heard of Max Lorraine.

STEVE: Eventually, the organisation was smashed, but Lorraine had laid his plans very carefully and he escaped. (*She hesitates*)

TEMPLE: Please go on ...

STEVE: From the very first moment that Richard was assigned to the Blakeley case, he had an uneasy feeling at the back of his mind, that he was up

30

against Max Lorraine. I saw him a few days before the accident, and he told me then that he was almost certain that Max Lorraine was the real influence behind The Front Page Men. (*A tiny pause*) I think the poor dear was a little worried – and rather frightened.

TEMPLE: Had your brother discussed with Sir Graham, or any of his colleagues, his theory regarding this man ... Lorraine?

STEVE: No. No, I don't think so.

TEMPLE: Why not?

STEVE: Because Richard had never actually met Lorraine, and Max Lorraine is hardly the sort of person one can talk about and sound convincing. He's like a character snatched from the most sensational thriller and inspired with a strange, almost satanic, intellect. (*Suddenly*) You think that sounds silly, don't you?

TEMPLE: (*Smiling*) Well, it sounds a little unusual! (*Picking up the ashtray from the small table and extinguishing his cigarette*) I can't begin to tell you how sorry I am about Richard ...

STEVE: (*With a faint smile*) He had a very great admiration for you. It was Richard who persuaded me to start the 'Send For Paul Temple' campaign in the Evening Post.

TEMPLE: (*Laughing*) Then by Timothy, you certainly started something! (*Seriously*) You know, it seems to me that your brother must have known something about Lorraine. Something which was indirectly responsible for his death.

STEVE: Yes. (*Slowly*) And two days before he died, Richard passed that information on to me.

TEMPLE: (*Surprised*) To you …? (*After a slight hesitation*) That may mean … danger. Great danger! You realise that?

STEVE: (*Softly*) Yes.

A slight pause.

TEMPLE: What is it you know about … Max Lorraine?

STEVE: (*Slowly*) I know that he has a small scar above the right elbow, that he smokes Russian cigarettes and is devoted to a girl who calls herself … Diana Fresnay.

TEMPLE: Diana Fresnay … (*There is a slight pause*) Miss Trent, you overheard my conversation with Sir Graham, was that the first time you'd heard of Dr Brightman?

STEVE: Yes. I was under the impression that Blakeley only had one visitor the day the child was kidnapped.

TEMPLE: You mean … Goldie? (*STEVE nods. After a slight pause*) You said you wanted my help. You said you wanted my help more than you've ever wanted anything in your life before … What did you mean by that?

STEVE: I meant, that from now on, I want it to be Paul Temple … versus … Max Lorraine!

There is a tiny pause, then suddenly TEMPLE smiles …

STEVE: (*Surprised*) Why are you smiling?

TEMPLE: I was just thinking of something Pryce said.

STEVE: (*Puzzled*) Pryce …?

TEMPLE: He said: You simply wouldn't take "No" for an answer.

STEVE smiles and holds out her hand. TEMPLE is about to take it, then hesitates. He turns towards the alcove.

STEVE: (*Astonished*) What is it?

TEMPLE: Listen!

There is a pause.

32

From the adjoining room can be heard the sound of a piano.
It is being played softly and with almost a strange charm.
PRYCE enters.

PRYCE: I beg your pardon, sir, but would you care …

TEMPLE: (*Interrupting PRYCE*) Pryce, is that someone in
              the library?

PRYCE: (*Rather surprised*) Why, yes, sir! It's the piano
              tuner. He called while you were with Sir Graham.
              I didn't wish to disturb you.

STEVE turns towards TEMPLE, a flicker of astonishment
crossing her face.

TEMPLE: The piano tuner?

PRYCE: Yes, sir. Mr Goldie. A … Mr J. P. Goldie.

TEMPLE and STEVE stand quite motionless. The piano
continues.

CURTAIN

END OF ACT 1

ACT TWO
SCENE ONE

The same as Scene 2, Act 1. The Lounge of Paul Temple's Flat.

It is the continuation of the preceding scene and at the rise of the curtain, TEMPLE, STEVE and PRYCE are all in the same positions as at the curtain of Act 1.

The piano can be heard.

There is a pause.

TEMPLE: (*Quietly*) Please tell Mr Goldie that I would rather like to have a word with him, Pryce.

The piano stops.

PRYCE: Very good, sir.

Exit PRYCE.

STEVE is about to speak but with a quick gesture TEMPLE stops her.

There is a tense pause.

PRYCE re-enters.

PRYCE: (*Announcing*) Mr Goldie, sir.

Exit PRYCE.

MR GOLDIE enters. He is a timid little man of about sixty. He carries a small and somewhat dilapidated attaché case.

GOLDIE: (*Nervously*) Did you wish to see me about something, Mr Temple? (*He remains standing near the alcove, obviously rather embarrassed*)

TEMPLE: (*Pleasantly*) Come along in, Mr Goldie. (*Shaking hands*) I don't think we've had the pleasure of meeting before?

34

GOLDIE: No, sir. (*Placing the attaché case on the floor*) I came to tune the piano last November, if I remember rightly, but you were abroad. Switzerland, I think your man said.

TEMPLE: Ah, yes. Switzerland!

GOLDIE: (*Smiling*) It's a rare pleasure, Mr Temple. I've often wanted to have the privilege of meeting you.

TEMPLE: You're very kind. Oh, this is a friend of mine ... Miss Trent.

STEVE: How do you do?

GOLDIE: (*With a jerky little bow*) How do you do, miss.

TEMPLE: Well, the fact of the matter is, Mr Goldie, I've been seriously thinking of changing my piano.

GOLDIE: (*Politely*) Really, Mr Temple?

TEMPLE: Yes. A friend of mine has a Remingstein for sale, and I must confess I'm very attracted towards it.

GOLDIE: (*Quietly*) A Remingstein? (*Shaking his head rather sadly*) I can't honestly advise you to make the change, Mr Temple.

TEMPLE: Oh?

GOLDIE: (*With a faint smile*) Now, if it had been a Bluthner, that would have been a different story.

TEMPLE: What don't you like about the Remingstein?

GOLDIE: Frankly, I've always found them so very unreliable. I was originally at Clapshaw and Thompson's in Regent Street, you know, and we had a great deal of trouble with the Remingstein people.

TEMPLE: (*Politely*) Is that so? (*Brightly*) Well, I'm certainly very glad I spoke to you. (*To STEVE*) It looks as if I might have made a pretty bad deal.

STEVE: (*Playing up to TEMPLE*) It does rather!

TEMPLE: Can I get you a drink, Mr Goldie? A glass of sherry perhaps ...?

35

GOLDIE: Thank you, Mr Temple, but I never drink during the day. As a matter of fact, I very rarely drink at all nowadays. (*To STEVE*) Asthma, you know.

STEVE: Oh, I'm sorry. (*With a smile*) About the asthma, I mean.

GOLDIE: I suppose you're very busy on a new novel, Mr Temple?

TEMPLE: Yes. I hope to have it completed by the end of the month.

GOLDIE: I loved that last book of yours, it was really most ingenious. How ever do you think of such things?

STEVE: Are you a great reader, Mr Goldie?

GOLDIE: Oh yes, very. We all are in our family, Miss. Always have been. My father was a great reader too. I don't ever remember seeing him without a book in his hand. (*Almost as an afterthought*) He once met Mark Twain, you know.

TEMPLE: (*Politely*) Really?

GOLDIE: Yes. He never tired of telling us about it. Although I don't think a great deal happened. (*With a rather wistful smile*) It was at a garden party.

TEMPLE: I see. (*After a tiny pause*) Have you read 'The Front Page Men'?

GOLDIE: (*Slowly turning towards TEMPLE*) 'The Front Page Men'? No. No, I'm afraid I haven't. They say it's very good.

TEMPLE: Yes.

GOLDIE: (*To STEVE*) I feel almost too frightened to read it. I mean, what with all these frightful robberies happening, and this shocking case of Sir Norman Blakeley's. Although, I suppose one can hardly hold the dear lady who wrote the book responsible?

36

STEVE: (*Smiling*) Hardly.

GOLDIE: (*Picking up his attaché case*) Well, if you take my tip, Mr Temple, you won't part with your piano. Certainly not in exchange for a Remingstein!

TEMPLE: I shall most certainly take your advice, Mr Goldie.

GOLDIE: (*To STEVE*) Good afternoon, miss.

STEVE: Good afternoon.

GOLDIE: (*Shaking hands*) Good afternoon, sir.

TEMPLE: Goodbye, Mr Goldie. (*He moves over to the alcove and goes out with GOLDIE*)

TEMPLE re-enters.

STEVE: Well, Mr Goldie certainly appears to be a harmless little man!

TEMPLE: Yes, quite a character I should imagine. (*Thoughtfully*) Miss Trent, I've been thinking … in view of what you've told me about Max Lorraine, I really feel that you ought to have a chat with the Assistant Commissioner. Apart from anything else, the facts which you have in your possession place you in danger. Possibly in very great danger.

STEVE: Yes, but that's why I came to see you, Mr Temple!

TEMPLE: (*Faintly amused*) Yes. Yes, I know. And don't worry, I shan't let you down.

STEVE: (*Rather pleased*) You're very sweet! (*She rises*) I'm afraid I've stayed rather longer than I expected.

TEMPLE and STEVE cross extreme right.

TEMPLE: You don't happen to know whether Richard had any papers? I mean, personal papers … letters … a diary … or anything of that nature?

TEMPLE and STEVE go out right through the alcove.

PRYCE enters from the right and crosses centre and shakes the cushions on the settee. He then moves across to the armchair near the radiogram.

TEMPLE re-enters.

PRYCE: (*Turning: apologetically*) I'm very sorry about this afternoon, sir.

TEMPLE: This afternoon?

PRYCE: The reporter, sir! I hadn't the slightest idea that the young lady was in the flat, sir. Naturally, I was under the impression that …

A bell rings.

TEMPLE: (*Interrupting PRYCE*) That's all right, Pryce.

The bell rings again.

TEMPLE: (*Glancing at his watch*) I rather imagine that's Chubby Wilson.

PRYCE: Yes, sir.

PRYCE goes out.

There is a slight pause.

PRYCE re-enters together with CHUBBY WILSON.

PRYCE: (*Staring at CHUBBY with obvious disapproval*) Mr Wilson, sir.

Exit PRYCE.

CHUBBY WILSON is a tough little man, elaborately overdressed.

CHUBBY:(*Nodding towards the alcove*) Can't understand why you keep that dressed-up monkey, guv'nor. Reminds me of Burton's window every time I set eyes on 'im.

TEMPLE: (*Laughing*) He's better for knowing. Well, you look fit, Chubby. How's the world been treating you?

CHUBBY: No complaints, Mr Temple. No complaints.

TEMPLE: Still in the 'dope' racket?

CHUBBY: (*Shocked*) Mr Temple!!!

TEMPLE: All right, Chubby, we'll skip the part about going straight!

CHUBBY:(*Rather nervously*) What is it you wanted to see me about …?

TEMPLE: (*Casually*) Oh, yes … What do you know about … The Front Page Men …?

CHUBBY: (*Alarmed*) Nothin' … Nothin' at all!

TEMPLE: All right, Chubby! All right! …

CHUBBY:(*Endeavouring to change the subject*) I'm going to America at the end of the week, Mr Temple. Wonderful country, America.

TEMPLE: Chubby, you haven't answered my question.

CHUBBY: What question?

TEMPLE: (*After a slight pause*) What do you know about The Front Page Men?

CHUBBY:I've told you – nothin'! Why the 'ell should I know anything about 'em? Listen, Mr Temple … I've been a lot of things in my time, but if there's one thing about me that's praiseworthy …

TEMPLE: There isn't, so you can cut the cackle! You're a dirty-minded little crook with about as much backbone as a filleted plaice! (*Smiling*) But I like you, Chubby. (*Slight pause*) Now listen … I want information and I'm willing to pay for it.

CHUBBY: How much?

TEMPLE: (*Amused*) That's better.

CHUBBY: (*Suspiciously*) Mind you, I don't say I've anything to tell …

TEMPLE: (*Quietly*) Listen, Chubby, you know me … you know that you can trust me.

CHUBBY: Oh, sure, Mr Temple, but …

TEMPLE: (*Softly*) Who are … The Front Page Men?

CHUBBY: (*After a slight hesitation*) I don't know. Nobody knows …

TEMPLE: But you've had dealings with them?

A slight pause.

CHUBBY: (*Nodding*) Yes … once. (*Looking up, rather nervously*) Mr Temple, have you heard of 'Amashyer'?

TEMPLE: 'Amashyer'? No, Chubby, I haven't. What is it?

CHUBBY: It's a drug.

TEMPLE: (*Thoughtfully*) A drug? What effect does it have?

CHUBBY: It makes people forget things … for a time at any rate.

TEMPLE: (*Thoughtfully*) M'm – Go on, Chubby …

CHUBBY: Well, I was in the Seamen's Hostel one night, having a game of cards, when up comes a fellow by the name of Danny Muller.

TEMPLE: (*Nodding*) Yes, I've heard of Muller.

CHUBBY: Well, Muller gave me a note and so far as I can remember it said: "Be at Redhouse Wharf tonight at nine" … To cut a long story short, I turned up at the wharf. There was a motorboat waiting for me and it took me to a sort of warehouse place on the river. There was a big bloke at the warehouse – a la-de-da sort of chap – and he said he wanted as much of this Amashyer drug as I could get him. I told him it was a pretty dangerous business trying to peddle dope, but all he did was to put his hand in his overcoat pocket and take out a wad of notes. There was three 'undred quid!

TEMPLE: (*Quietly*) Where is this warehouse, Chubby?

CHUBBY: (*Rather puzzled*) Blessed if I know. So far as I could gather it took us about an hour from Redhouse Wharf.

TEMPLE: I see. (*Suddenly*) Well, thanks, Chubby, you've been a great help.

40

CHUBBY:(*Nervously*) I say, listen, guv'nor, I don't know what the game is, but if you intend picking up Danny Muller, I'd consider it a favour if you'd leave it over for three or four days.

TEMPLE: Why?

CHUBBY: Well, Danny's a funny sort of cove. If he thought I'd been talking out of turn, he ... he might get ideas into his head.

TEMPLE: And will three or four days make a difference?

CHUBBY: (*Nodding*) Well, I'm sailing on the Laconia on Thursday.

TEMPLE: (*Rather surprised*) Then you really are going to the States? (*Taking out his wallet*) Well, by rights, I suppose I ought to send the F.B.I. a cable. (*Smiling*) Still, I reckon they'll soon find out for themselves what a double-crossing little blackguard you are! (*He takes a note from his wallet*) Here you are, Chubby.

CHUBBY: (*Smiling*) Thanks, guv'nor! (*He looks at the note, and holds it up to the light*) Blimey, fifty quid ... I thought it was a tenner!

Enter PRYCE. He glances at CHUBBY and gives a slow smile of satisfaction before turning towards TEMPLE.

PRYCE: The Assistant Commissioner and Inspector Hunter have called, sir.

CHUBBY:(*Staggered*) What! (*He moves towards TEMPLE*) What the 'ell does this mean? If this is a blarsted trap I'll ...

TEMPLE: (*Amused*) It's all right, Chubby. There's nothing to get excited about. (*To PRYCE*) In a few minutes, Pryce.

PRYCE: Yes, sir.

Exit PRYCE.

CHUBBY: (*Apprehensively*) I want to get out of 'ere! I want to get out of 'ere bloody quick!

TEMPLE: (*Amused, crossing towards the bookcase*) All right, Chubby, all right … (*He presses the button, and the panel opens*) If you take this lift, it'll bring you into the basement. The door facing the entrance leads into Milford Street.

CHUBBY: (*Surprised*) Oh! (*Smiling*) Oh, thanks, guv'nor. (*He holds out his hand*) Give my love to the Commissioner and Inspector – er …

TEMPLE: Hunter. (*He shakes hands*)

CHUBBY: Hunter? (*Puzzled*) He's one of the new crowd, isn't he?

TEMPLE: That's right. Straight from college.

CHUBBY: (*Entering the lift*) I'll send him a postcard from Hollywood – just to encourage the boy!

TEMPLE: Make sure it isn't Alcatraz, Chubby.

CHUBBY: (*Winking*) Not me, guv'nor. I got friends in Washington.

TEMPLE: (*Laughing*) Goodbye, Chubby! (*He closes the panel and returns centre*)

PRYCE re-enters followed by SIR GRAHAM and HUNTER.

PRYCE: Sir Graham Forbes and Inspector Hunter, sir.

Exit PRYCE.

TEMPLE: (*Advancing towards the alcove*) Hello, Sir Graham! I'm glad you've returned. I want to have a chat with you.

FORBES: (*Obviously depressed*) You know Inspector Hunter I believe?

TEMPLE: (*Shaking hands*) Yes, rather! (*To FORBES*) What happened about Blakeley?

FORBES: He was dead, all right. They picked him up from the bank early this morning and dumped him in the telephone box. (*Crossing towards the cocktail*

42

cabinet) Do you mind if I have a drink, Temple? God knows, I need one!

TEMPLE: No, of course not. Help yourself, Sir Graham. (*To HUNTER*) What'll you have, Hunter?

HUNTER: Nothing for me … thanks.

TEMPLE: How do you know Blakeley was picked up from the bank?

FORBES: (*Mixing himself a whisky and soda*) Because I had a man trailing him, and the damn fool bungled the job!

TEMPLE: But who picked him up?

FORBES: (*Thoughtfully*) I don't know.

TEMPLE: Could it have been Brightman?

FORBES: (*Surprised*) Brightman? Yes. Yes, I suppose it could have been. (*Puzzled*) Why do you ask?

TEMPLE: (*Quietly*) I wondered, that's all.

There is a slight pause.

FORBES: (*After drinking*) Ever since this business first started, there's been a definite campaign, both in the newspapers and amongst a certain section of the public, urging us to … er …

HUNTER: (*Smiling*) Send for Paul Temple?

FORBES: (*Nodding*) Yes, Hunter. To … er … send for Paul Temple. (*Slightly irritated*) Well, I don't mind telling you, Temple, the whole damned campaign got me rattled! I was pretty firmly convinced, in my own mind at any rate, that there was nothing you could possibly do to … er … assist us in this matter. Now, however, I'm not so sure. (*He finishes his drink and replaces the glass on the cocktail cabinet*)

TEMPLE: But why the change of attitude, Sir Graham? Because of what's happened to Blakeley?

FORBES: No, not entirely.

43

SIR GRAHAM looks across at HUNTER and nods, as if granting permission for the INSPECTOR to speak.

HUNTER: (*Quietly*) Temple, you've heard of the Falkirk diamond?

TEMPLE: Why of course! Who hasn't? (*Casually*) Isn't it on show in Regent Street, or somewhere?

HUNTER: It <u>was</u> on show in Regent Street ... yes.

TEMPLE: (*Slowly, rather puzzled*) It was on show? (*Suddenly*) Good God, you don't mean to say ... the ... Front Page Men ...?

FORBES: (*Nodding*) This afternoon ... at four-thirty. They smashed the front of the jewellers to pieces ... and killed two onlookers. (*Ominously*) But they got the diamond!

TEMPLE: Four thirty? You mean while ...

HUNTER: Yes, while we were watching the telephone box. (*Bitterly*) Rather clever, wasn't it?

FORBES: Hunter seems to think that we're up against a super-man! A genius, with an unusual flair for criminal organisation! And by God, I'm not so sure he isn't right!

TEMPLE: (*Smiling*) After you left the flat this afternoon, I had several visitors, Sir Graham.

FORBES: Oh?

TEMPLE motions HUNTER into a chair. SIR GRAHAM sits on the arm of the settee.

TEMPLE: The first was a girl. A girl by the name of Steve Trent.

FORBES: (*Amused*) We know Miss Trent, all right. She happens to be a reporter on The Evening Post.

TEMPLE: Yes. She also happens to be Richard Harvey's sister.

FORBES: (*Rising*) What! (*Incredulously*) Harvey's sister ...

HUNTER: But that's impossible!

44

TEMPLE: (*Pleasantly*) I don't think so, Inspector. (*To FORBES*) Miss Trent also shares the same opinion as Hunter, Sir Graham. She feels quite convinced that The Front Page Men are under the direct control of one man – a man by the name of Max Lorraine.

FORBES: Max Lorraine? But why hasn't Miss Trent discussed this matter with us?

TEMPLE: I think she's had a very good reason for not doing so. However, I believe I've now persuaded her to come along and have a chat with you. (*Suddenly*) Incidentally, have they returned the Blakeley child?

FORBES: Yes, thank God! A message came through from the house about an hour ago.

HUNTER: Is he all right, sir?

FORBES: (*Slightly puzzled*) He seems to be all right, except for the fact that he can't remember anything. (*Thoughtfully*) I wonder if it's some kind of drug they're using? (*To HUNTER*) You might tell Mac to let 'Doc' Henderson have a look at the Blakeley boy.

HUNTER: Yes, sir.

TEMPLE: (*Quietly*) They're using a drug called Amashyer, Sir Graham. It's not very well known in this country.

FORBES: Amashyer? (*Rather surprised*) I've certainly never heard of it before!

HUNTER: How do you know that they're using this drug, Temple?

TEMPLE: (*Smiling*) I had the information on very good authority, Inspector, I assure you.

FORBES: (*Rather intrigued*) On very good authority?

45

TEMPLE: After the visit of Miss Trent, I had a caller who, *(Smiling)* for reasons which I am sure you would both appreciate, I should prefer to be nameless. However, he placed one or two rather interesting facts at my disposal. Firstly, he had had direct contact with The Front Page Men, and secondly, he was convinced that the organisation have their headquarters on the river, quite possibly in a deserted warehouse.

FORBES: A deserted warehouse!

TEMPLE: Well, he claims that on one occasion he was taken from Redhouse Wharf to the warehouse, although I must confess that he seemed extremely hazy as to its exact whereabouts.

FORBES: *(Excited)* My God, Temple! This is most important!

SIR GRAHAM crosses to the telephone on the small table, lifts the receiver, and dials.

HUNTER: *(To FORBES; rather excited)* If this information is correct, they'll obviously try to get the Falkirk diamond to the hide-out as soon as possible!

FORBES: Yes. Yes, of course! *(Suddenly: at the telephone)* Hello? This is the Assistant Commissioner speaking … please put me through to Chief Inspector Reid. *(A tiny pause)* Thank you.

TEMPLE opens the cigarette box on the small table but discovers that it is empty. HUNTER notices this and takes out his cigarette case.

HUNTER: Have one of mine, Temple.

TEMPLE: *(Taking a cigarette)* Oh, thanks!

HUNTER: *(Turning with the cigarette case towards SIR GRAHAM)* Cigarette, sir?

FORBES: No, thank you, Hunter. *(On the phone)* Is that you, Mac? … Forbes here. Listen! I want you to get hold of Inspector Brooks at Kingston … Yes, Brooks! I want a launch at North Pier … Tonight … Nine sharp … I shall want Donovan, and Lewis. Is that clear? … Yes. Yes, that's right … I don't see why not … Yes, O.K. … (*He turns from the telephone*)

HUNTER: (*Replacing his cigarette case*) Does that mean …?

FORBES: (*Grimly determined*) It means that whatever happens, we've got to find that warehouse, Hunter! (*To TEMPLE*) It might be a good idea if you came along with us.

TEMPLE: (*Smiling*) Why not?

FORBES: We'll pick you up at about eight-thirty; will that be all right?

TEMPLE: Perfectly. (*He crosses to the bell push*)

FORBES: (*To HUNTER*) I want you to get back to Regent Street, Hunter. (*To TEMPLE*) There's going to be hell to pay over this Falkirk business.

HUNTER: Yes, sir.

HUNTER shakes hands with TEMPLE.

HUNTER: Goodbye, Temple.

TEMPLE: Goodbye.

FORBES: (*To HUNTER*) You can drop me at the Yard first. (*Shaking hands with TEMPLE*) We'll meet tonight.

PRYCE enters.

TEMPLE: Yes. (*To PRYCE*) Sir Graham and Inspector Hunter are leaving, Pryce.

PRYCE: Very good, sir.

Exit SIR GRAHAM and HUNTER through the alcove, followed by PRYCE.

PAUL TEMPLE crosses to the bookcase and takes a rather heavy volume from the top shelf. He crosses and takes the cigarette lighter from the small table. TEMPLE places the book on the arm of the settee and as he lights his cigarette slowly turns the pages.

After a little while it occurs to him that there is something unfamiliar with the cigarette; he takes it from his mouth, glances at the name on the cigarette, and then with rather a puzzled frown turns towards the alcove through which INSPECTOR HUNTER has recently departed.

CURTAIN
END OF SCENE 1

ACT TW0
SCENE TWO

SCENE: A warehouse near Redhouse Wharf.   12.30am –
the same night.

It is a storeroom built over the river. At the back centre a
sloping ceiling gives way to a window looking out of a
private courtyard which runs parallel to the river.

The room is furnished: several chairs, a settee, a table, and a
small cocktail cabinet. The only light comes from a reading
lamp which stands by the side of the telephone on the table.
The furniture is scattered, and the general effect is rather that
of an untidy studio.

Down centre, a thick carpet conceals, in the floor, a sliding
trap door which lands, by means of a wooden stairway, to the
river. The entrance to the warehouse, other than by the trap
door, is off right. Fixed to one of the wooden beams above the
cocktail cabinet, and partly hidden by a carefully placed
gauze, is a red electrical bulb; this lights up immediately
anyone touches the stairway leading from the river.

*When the curtain rises, BRIGHTMAN is standing with his
back to the audience staring out of the window. Suddenly, the
sound of an approaching car is heard and the headlamp
beams flash across the window. BRIGHTMAN moves to the
left of the window anxiously staring down into the courtyard.
The headlights are switched off, and the engine stops.
BRIGHTMAN returns centre, hesitates for a second then
crosses over to the cocktail cabinet. From the side of the*

cocktail cabinet, he takes a small Gladstone bag which he places on the table.
DIANA FRESNAY enters from the right. She is tall, good-looking and very smartly dressed.

DIANA: Haven't the others arrived yet?

BRIGHTMAN: No.

DIANA: (*Smiling*) I'm sorry I'm late.

BRIGHTMAN: (*Impatiently*) I've been waiting almost an hour.

DIANA: You got my message all right?

BRIGHTMAN: About Chubby Wilson? (*He nods*)

DIANA: Was Jimmy surprised?

BRIGHTMAN: A little …

DIANA: (*Taking off her gloves*) You look worried, Andrew.

BRIGHTMAN: I feel it! Hellishly worried!

DIANA: Why?

BRIGHTMAN: You know perfectly well … why! (*He taps the bag*) This Blakeley business was a crazy stunt, if ever there was one!

DIANA: Crazy? (*Crossing to the cocktail cabinet*) What was so crazy about it? (*She mixes herself a drink*)

BRIGHTMAN: (*Taking a wad of notes from the bag*) This stuff is useless … it's so hot you daren't even look at it! (*He throws the notes back into the bag*)

DIANA: (*Smiling*) But we got the Falkirk diamond, and don't forget … that's what we were after.

BRIGHTMAN: Then why in hell's name didn't we go out after the diamond in the first place and leave the Blakeley kid alone? (*He takes the bag*

50

from the table) If you want my opinion, Max bungled the Blakeley job, and bungled it damn badly!

DIANA: That's interesting. I hope you'll tell him so.

BRIGHTMAN: (*Puzzled*) What do you mean?

DIANA finishes her drink and places the glass on the centre table.

There is a pause.

DIANA: We're going to have company tonight, Andrew … very distinguished company.

BRIGHTMAN: Distinguished company …? (*Surprised*) You don't mean that Max Lorraine is actually … coming … here?

DIANA: Yes.

BRIGHTMAN: But … why?

DIANA: The boys are restless. They've been working in the dark long enough. If they don't meet Max soon … there'll be trouble.

BRIGHTMAN: (*Excitedly*) Good God, haven't I been telling you that for the past six weeks! (*He drops the bag near the window*) I'm glad you've made him change his mind. It was a smart move, Diana.

BRIGHTMAN is obviously pleased.

DIANA: (*Thoughtfully*) I wonder. (*Suddenly*) I hope Jimmy understood about Chubby Wilson. Max seemed pretty anxious about it.

BRIGHTMAN: What's Max worried about? Chubby Wilson couldn't find this place in a thousand years. Danny only brought him here once, and that was …

DIANA: And that was once too often!

BRIGHTMAN: We had to have the Amashyer drug. There was no other way of getting it!

DIANA:	Well, Chubby's been talking …
BRIGHTMAN:	Talking? You mean to the 'Yard'?
DIANA:	No. To … Paul Temple …
BRIGHTMAN:	Temple! (*Anxiously*) My God, I hope Temple isn't going to interfere with our …
DIANA:	(*Smiling*) There's no need to worry about Temple. Max is going to take care of Paul Temple … and very soon.

There is a pause.

BRIGHTMAN:	Diana … why is Max coming here?
DIANA:	I've already told you.
BRIGHTMAN:	(*Shaking his head*) He's got a reason … a definite reason … hasn't he?
DIANA:	(*Smiling*) Yes.
BRIGHTMAN:	Well?
DIANA:	We're getting near the final curtain, Andrew.
BRIGHTMAN:	What do you mean?
DIANA:	One more job like the Falkirk diamond and we're sitting pretty.
BRIGHTMAN:	(*Emphatically*) They'll never do it! It's no use, Diana. I had a hell of a job to get Swan and Danny to agree over this Falkirk business.
DIANA:	They'll do it all right, when they hear what Max has got to say.
BRIGHTMAN:	(*Apprehensively*) What's … he got in mind?

A slight pause.

DIANA:	(*Quietly*) The Nurembourg Collection …
BRIGHTMAN:	(*Staggered*) The Nurembourg Collection! Good God, is the man crazy …? Why, it's worth the best part of a million.
DIANA:	(*With a faint smile*) I rather gather that's the attraction.

BRIGHTMAN: Max must be out of his mind to even think of such a thing! You'll never get the boys to …

DIANA: (*Scornfully*) They'll do exactly what they're told! Make no mistake about that!

BRIGHTMAN: (*Extracting his cigarette case*) I can't say I like the sound of this Paul Temple business. Temple isn't a fool by any stretch of the imagination. (*He lights his cigarette*)

DIANA: I've already assured you that Temple will be taken care of. Max isn't tolerating interference from anyone, not at a time like this. (*Softly, her eyes on BRIGHTMAN*) Remember … there's no one quite like Max Lorraine, anywhere … you can always be sure of that, Andrew.

BRIGHTMAN: (*After a slight pause*) You got the Blakeley child back, all right?

DIANA: Yes. There was no difficulty.

BRIGHTMAN: (*Smiling*) I told you about my visit to the 'Yard' didn't I?

DIANA nods.

BRIGHTMAN: That was a brilliant move. Although I must confess, I didn't agree with Max about it, not at first at any rate. (*Amused*) You should have seen Forbes' face when I mentioned …

The red light appears above the cocktail cabinet.

DIANA: The light!

BRIGHTMAN: (*Briskly*) Not before time either.

BRIGHTMAN stubs his cigarette in an ashtray on the table, then crosses centre. He removes the carpet and, by means of an iron ring in the floor, lifts the trap door. Immediately he does so, there is the sound of voices.

SWAN: (*Off*) Steady, Danny! Steady!

JIMMY: (*Off*) Take it easy, Swan! Take it easy!

JIMMY MILLS emerges through the trap door. He is slim and alert.

DIANA: (*Pleasantly*) Hello, Jimmy!

JIMMY: Hello, Lovely! How long have you been here?

DIANA: Not long.

JIMMY: (*To BRIGHTMAN*) You look bright, doc, I must say!

BRIGHTMAN: You're hellishly late!

JIMMY: (*Insolently*) Yes, and we've had a hell of a lot to put up with!

DANNY MULLER and SWAN WILLIAMS enter through the trap door from the river. DANNY is shorter than JIMMY and not nearly so self-possessed. SWAN is an American. He is tall, and tough and rather wiry.

SWAN: Boy … what a night!

DANNY: Hello, doc …

BRIGHTMAN: Where's Lucky?

DANNY: He's coming. (*Wiping his mouth with his sleeve*) My Gawd, I'm thirsty …

SWAN: You said it, Danny! (*He crosses to the cocktail cabinet*)

BRIGHTMAN: (*Slightly impatient*) Well, what happened?

JIMMY: What happened …? (*He laughs*)

SWAN: Say, what didn't happen!

DIANA: (*To SWAN*) You got … Wilson?

SWAN: Sure. (*He comes down centre with his drink*)

DANNY and JIMMY MILLS are at the cocktail cabinet.

JIMMY: (*To DIANA*) Swan picked up Chubby Wilson at Maynard's Club on the Tottenham Court Road. We brought him down to the river and dumped him at the spot near …

54

BRIGHTMAN: (*Irritated*) Dumped him! How the devil do you know he won't …

JIMMY: (*Coolly*) Chubby was out before he hit the water. Lucky saw to that all right.

DANNY: The poor devil was spark out, doc. No mistakes about that … you can take my word for it.

JIMMY: (*Coming down centre*) What's all the fuss about …? I never thought Chubby Wilson was a bad little squirt. (*With a shrug*) Maybe he talked a bit too much, but …

BRIGHTMAN: That's just the point. He talked too much and too often.

JIMMY: What do you mean?

DIANA: Chubby Wilson came here one night, remember, Jimmy?

JIMMY: (*Thoughtfully*) Yes. Yes, that's right.

DANNY: (*Suddenly*) My God, you don't mean to say he started blabbing …?

DIANA nods.

JIMMY: Then that accounts for the river patrol. I knew darn well there was something fishy.

BRIGHTMAN: River patrol …?

JIMMY: We had quite a lively time tonight, doc. Pity you weren't with us.

SWAN: If you ask me things are getting hot. Maybe a bit too hot to be healthy.

LUCKY GIBSON enters through the trap door. He is a tough little cockney.

LUCKY: 'Ello, doc! (*To DIANA*) Didn't expect to see you, Di.

DIANA: (*Smiling*) I do wish you wouldn't call me Di.

DANNY: (*At the cocktail cabinet*) What'll you have?

55

LUCKY: Something with a kick, Danny. I need it
                after monkeying about with that blasted
                Tommy gun!

*LUCKY closes the trap door and JIMMY moves the carpet
into position. LUCKY crosses to the cocktail cabinet.*

DANNY: (*Offering a drink*) Here … we … are …

LUCKY: Thanks, china! (*He raises his glass*) Good
                'ealth everybody! (*He drinks*)

DANNY: (*Amused*) How's that?

LUCKY: (*Gasping for breath*) Strewth!

JIMMY: (*To BRIGHTMAN*) What happened to the
                Blakeley money …?

SWAN: Yeah … what happened to that dough you
                picked up from Blakeley?

BRIGHTMAN: It's here … (*He points to the bag*)

DANNY: (*Delighted*) Well … what are we waiting
                for? (*He picks up the bag*)

BRIGHTMAN: (*Impatiently*) Are you crazy? (*Taking the
                bag from DANNY*) This stuff is hot … red
                hot!

SWAN: Sure! It's worse than snide. The numbers
                have been dropped from Putney to
                Plymouth!

DANNY: What d'you mean?

JIMMY: (*Quietly*) The doc's right, Danny. We can't
                touch it.

DANNY: Then what are we going to do? (*To
                BRIGHTMAN*) Where's our cut coming
                from?

BRIGHTMAN: From the Falkirk pay off …

DANNY: That's going to take time.

LUCKY: An' a 'ell of a long time if you arsks me.

SWAN: Things are getting pretty tight, Brightman.
                We need the dough.

BRIGHTMAN:	Lorraine is going to handle the Falkirk diamond – the money should be through inside of a month. You'll each get the best part of six hundred.
LUCKY:	(*Pleased*) Six hundred …
JIMMY:	(*Truculently*) And what does … Max Lorraine get out of it?
DIANA:	(*Pleasantly*) I should ask him, Jimmy.
SWAN:	What d'you mean … ask him? You know darn well we've never set eyes on the guy.
DIANA:	But you will …
JIMMY:	(*Surprised*) We … will …?
DANNY:	When?

There is a pause.

DIANA:	Tonight.
DANNY:	(*Astounded*) Tonight!
JIMMY:	(*Bewildered*) You mean the Chief is actually coming here … tonight?

DIANA nods.

SWAN:	Then he must have a reason. A pretty good reason too, the way I figure things.
BRIGHTMAN:	(*To SWAN*) You've heard of the Nurembourg Collection?
SWAN:	The Nurembourg Collection? Why, sure! Who hasn't?
JIMMY:	According to the newspapers, the collection was brought over from New York on Thursday and taken down to Lord Romer's … place … just … outside … of Guildford. (*He stops speaking and stares at DIANA with astonishment*)
DIANA:	What's the matter?
JIMMY:	Good God, you don't mean he expects us to lift the Nurembourg Collection?

SWAN: If he does, here's one picaninny who's not playing ball …

DIANA: (*With a smile*) We shall see, Swan!

The red light appears.

DANNY: The light, Jimmy!

LUCKY: (*Alarmed*) It's the cops! (*He takes a revolver from his pocket and moves across right*)

BRIGHTMAN: Stay where you are, Lucky! (*He looks at DIANA*) Is this … Lorraine?

The red light goes off, then flicks off and on rather suddenly.

DIANA: Yes.

There is a tiny pause.

DANNY: (*Nervously*) The Chief …

JIMMY: (*Apprehensively*) Front Page Man … No 1 …

BRIGHTMAN crosses centre and removes the carpet and lifts the trap door. JIMMY joins LUCKY and DANNY on the far side of the carpet. SWAN is on the extreme left. They are apprehensive and curious.

DIANA advances to the trap door. She smiles as the shadow of the new arrival falls across the entrance.

DIANA: We've been waiting for you, Max.

But we do not see Max Lorraine for as the shadow lengthens the curtain descends.

CURTAIN
END OF SCENE TWO

ACT TWO
SCENE THREE

SCENE: Same as Scene 1, Act 2. The lounge of Paul Temple's flat. It is three-thirty the following afternoon.

When the curtain rises the room is deserted.

TEMPLE enters through the alcove and is followed by PRYCE. TEMPLE is wearing an overcoat and carrying a hat and a pair of gloves. He crosses to the small table on which there are several unopened letters.

TEMPLE: Has anyone called, Pryce? (*He is looking at one or two of the letters*)

PRYCE: Yes, sir. Mr Mitchell called at about one-thirty and Mr Goldie at about a quarter to three.

TEMPLE: (*Surprised*) Mr Goldie? (*He replaces the letters on the table*) Have you any idea what he wanted?

PRYCE: I couldn't say, sir. He waited about a quarter of an hour and then left.

TEMPLE: (*Briskly; taking off his overcoat*) Yes, all right, Pryce.

PRYCE: (*Taking the overcoat, hat and gloves*) Thank you, sir. (*He crosses towards the alcove but suddenly turns*) Oh, I was forgetting, sir. Miss Trent rang up for the second time about half-an-hour ago and asked what time you'd be in. I said about three-thirty. She telephoned this morning, sir, just after you left.

TEMPLE: Thank you, Pryce.

Exit PRYCE.

The telephone rings and TEMPLE lifts the receiver.

TEMPLE: Hello? … Yes … Paul Temple speaking … Oh, hello, Sir Graham! … Yes … Pardon? … Four-thirty? I should say that would do splendidly … No, I'm afraid I haven't… (*Suddenly*) Oh, Sir Graham … I had a word with Reid this morning about a man called Muller …M'm? Yes, Danny Muller … I advised Mac to get a warrant out for him … (*Tiny pause*) I'm afraid I couldn't before, Sir Graham, I gave Chubby Wilson my word that nothing would be said until … M'm? (*Amused*) You catch the bird, Sir Graham, I'll make him talk! … Yes … Yes, all right. Goodbye. (*He replaces the receiver, glances at the wristlet watch, then crosses over to the cocktail cabinet*)

While TEMPLE is mixing himself a whisky and soda, he notices a small pocket flask near the decanter, he takes the flask and places it in his hip pocket. Somewhat thoughtfully, he returns centre with his drink.

PRYCE enters.

TEMPLE: What is it, Pryce?

PRYCE: Miss Trent has called, sir.

TEMPLE: (*Nodding*) Yes, all right, Pryce.

Exit PRYCE. He re-enters, carrying a small flat parcel, and followed by STEVE TRENT.

PRYCE: (*Announcing*) Miss Trent, sir.

STEVE: (*Shaking hands*) Hello! I do hope I haven't dropped in at an awkward moment?

TEMPLE: No, of course not. I've been expecting you. (*Smiling*) I promised Sir Graham that we'd see him at about four-thirty.

STEVE: Four-thirty?

TEMPLE: Is that going to be difficult for you?

STEVE: Well, I'm afraid it is going to be just a shade awkward. I promised to be back at the office by

60

about four-fifteen. (*Suddenly*) I daresay I could be at the Yard by about five, if that would be all right?

TEMPLE: I think I might quite possibly keep the Assistant Commissioner entertained for half an hour or so. (*Noticing PRYCE is still there*) Yes – what is it, Pryce?

PRYCE: I beg your pardon, sir, but this package arrived this afternoon by district messenger.

TEMPLE: (*Crossing over and taking the parcel*) Oh, thank you. (*He returns centre*)

Exit PRYCE.

TEMPLE: (*Looking at the parcel*) Excuse me.

STEVE: Yes, of course.

TEMPLE: (*Unwrapping the package*) I haven't the remotest idea what this is!

The package contains an ordinary twelve-inch gramophone record.

STEVE: (*Smiling*) Did you order it?

TEMPLE: (*Amused*) No, there must be some mistake! (*Looking at the paper wrapping*) It's addressed to me all right.

STEVE: (*Pleasantly: taking the record from TEMPLE*) What's it called? (*She looks at the label and her expression hardens*)

TEMPLE: What's the matter?

STEVE: (*Touching the label*) Look!

TEMPLE: (*Leaning over STEVE's shoulder and reading*) For Paul Temple … from … The Front Page Men …

There is a slight pause.

TEMPLE: (*Taking the record*) Stay where you are! (*He turns towards the radiogram*)

STEVE: What are you going to do?

TEMPLE: I'm going to play it. (*He switches the set on*) It takes a little time to warm up.

STEVE: (*Puzzled*) What do you think is on the record?

TEMPLE: (*Holding the record rather gently*) I don't know, most probably a message or … (*He stops speaking, obviously deep in thought*)

STEVE: (*Puzzled*) What is it?

TEMPLE: (*Looking at the record*) I'm afraid I was being just a little bit too … obvious. (*He returns centre*)

STEVE: Obvious?

TEMPLE: (*With a faint smile*) Supposing you sent someone a gramophone record. It had no official label and looked very mysterious. What do you think would be the first thing you'd do with it?

STEVE: Why, play it, of course. That's what everyone would do …

TEMPLE: Yes, of course it is. (*Thoughtfully*) That's what everyone would do …

STEVE: (*Puzzled*) I don't understand?

TEMPLE: The person who sent this record knew that I'd be puzzled by it, and he knew, without a shadow of doubt, that the first thing I should want to do would be to satisfy my curiosity by playing it.

STEVE: Well?

TEMPLE: (*Rather excited*) Don't you see? That's the whole point! The Front Page Men want me to play this record, and immediately I do so their purpose in sending it to me is fulfilled.

STEVE: But … what is their purpose? Why should they send you a gramophone record? If it contains a message, then …

TEMPLE: (*Quietly*) But surely a message could have been sent to me in writing?

STEVE: Yes. Yes, I … suppose it could. (*Puzzled*) Then
            what's on the record?

TEMPLE: (*Softly; looking at the record*) Nothing … nothing
            of importance … I'm sure of that.

STEVE: (*Rather bewildered*) Then why should they send
            it? You said yourself their purpose was to get you
            to play it.

TEMPLE: (*Thoughtfully*) Yes. Yes, that's true.

*Deep in thought TEMPLE returns to the radiogram. He
stands staring at the set. Suddenly his expression changes.*

TEMPLE: By Timothy! By Timothy, I've got it! The
            gramophone!!! (*He kneels down and looks at the
            grills on the front of the concealed speaker*)

STEVE: What is it?

TEMPLE: (*Thoughtfully; rather excited*) That's what they
            want … that's what they want, all right! (*Tapping
            the record*) This is a blind … they sent it to make
            sure I'd use the set. (*He straightens up*) The
            radio's been tampered with.

STEVE: (*Rising, and crossing towards the recess*) What do
            you mean?

TEMPLE: Look at the gauze on the speaker! Not only that
            … the set's been moved. I can tell by the carpet.

STEVE: (*Looking at the foot of the radiogram*) Yes.

TEMPLE: (*Quietly; rather grim*) My God! My God, I've got
            it!

STEVE: What is it?

TEMPLE: (*Taking STEVE by the arm and leading her away
            from the recess*) Stand on one side, Steve.
            (*Returning to front of the set*) Now look … (*His
            hand is just above the tone arm*) When I want to
            put a record on, I stand in front of the loudspeaker
            … like this …

STEVE: Yes.

TEMPLE: I lift the arm and bring it across to the record …
(*He indicates the movement without touching the tone arm*)

STEVE: (*Puzzled*) Yes, but I don't quite …

TEMPLE: (*Interrupting STEVE*) I'm going to do exactly the same, only I'm going to stand on one side instead – you'll see why in a minute!

TEMPLE stands to one side of the radiogram, making sure at the same time that STEVE is well back on the other side of the instrument. Then, very gingerly, he picks up the tone arm. He swings it over, as if to start the motor, just before setting the needle down on the groove of the record. During that fraction of a second the room is filled with a loud, deafening report. A wisp of acrid smoke begins to issue from the loudspeaker grille.

STEVE: (*Alarmed*) Paul … are … you all right?

TEMPLE: (*Crossing to the front of the radiogram*) Yes, I'm all right! (*He stoops down and examines the set*) There's a small revolver hidden by the speaker, it's been wired up with the tone arm. (*He rises*) Immediately the arm was moved, the revolver fired. (*Smiling*) Now you know why they sent me the gramophone record!

PRYCE enters.

PRYCE: (*Rather bewildered*) Is anything the matter, sir?

TEMPLE: No, it's all right.

PRYCE: I thought I heard a revolver shot, sir?

TEMPLE: (*Smiling*) There's nothing to worry about.

PRYCE: Very good, sir. (*He turns away*)

TEMPLE: (*Crossing centre*) Oh, Pryce!

PRYCE: (*Turning*) Yes, sir?

The flat bell rings.

TEMPLE: You say that Mr Goldie called this afternoon and waited for about a quarter of an hour?

PRYCE: Yes, sir.

TEMPLE: Was he alone?

PRYCE: (*Surprised*) Oh yes, sir!

TEMPLE: (*Dismissing PRYCE*) Thank you, Pryce.

Exit PRYCE.

STEVE: Goldie? (*Amazed*) Has Mr Goldie been here …
             today?

TEMPLE: Yes. Apparently, he called at about a quarter to
             three. I was out. I've been out since ten o'clock
             this morning.

STEVE: (*Nodding towards the radiogram*) You don't think
             he had anything to do with this …?

TEMPLE: (*Quietly*) I don't know.

PRYCE re-enters.

PRYCE: Beg your pardon, sir …

TEMPLE: What is it, Pryce?

PRYCE: Mr Mitchell has called again, sir. He seems very
             anxious to have a word with you.

TEMPLE: Ask him in here.

Exit PRYCE. He returns with GERALD MITCHELL.

PRYCE: (*Announcing*) Mr Mitchell, sir.

Exit PRYCE.

*GERALD is nervous and worried. He crosses towards
TEMPLE.*

TEMPLE: (*Shaking hands*) Hello, Gerald!

GERALD: Paul … something's happened … something
             rather important … (*He looks at STEVE*) I must …
             see … you alone …

TEMPLE: This is Miss Trent … It's all right, Gerald, you can
             talk.

STEVE: Perhaps I could wait in the library if Mr Mitchell
             would rather …

65

GERALD: No! No, it's all right … please forgive me. (*To TEMPLE*) I'm terribly sorry bursting in like this, Paul, but … it's about Ann.

TEMPLE: Ann …?

GERALD: She's … disappeared …

TEMPLE: Disappeared!!

GERALD: (*Desperately*) Paul, I'm serious! Damn serious! You've got to listen to me …

TEMPLE: (*Turning towards the cocktail cabinet*) Well?

GERALD: (*Pacing across the room*) Last night … I left Ann at The Savoy, and instead of going straight back to the flat, I went along to the office for a little while. When I arrived home, at about a quarter to one, I found a note on Ann's dressing table, saying that a friend of hers at St Albans – a girl called Stella White – has been taken seriously ill, and that Ann had promised to spend the night with her. This didn't worry me because I knew that Stella and Ann were very great friends. (*He hesitates*) This morning, however … a card arrived for Ann … it was from Stella and was posted in Cornwall.

STEVE: (*Surprised*) Cornwall!

GERALD: Yes. Apparently, Stella's on holiday – she's not expected back until the sixteenth.

TEMPLE: (*Quietly*) Then … Ann couldn't have gone to St Albans …?

GERALD: No … No … (*Suddenly alarmed*) But where is she? … Where is … she … Paul?

TEMPLE: What time did she actually leave the flat, do you know?

GERALD: The maid said about twenty past ten.

66

TEMPLE: (*Thoughtfully*) Twenty past ten … I see. (*Offering a drink*) I shouldn't worry too much, Gerald, after all there might be a perfectly simple explanation.

GERALD: (*Taking the whisky and soda*) My God, I hope so! Ann's been so very strange just recently. Although, I daresay I've been a pretty unbearable sort of devil to live with!

TEMPLE: Nonsense! (*Crosses to the bell-push and rings for PRYCE*) Miss Trent and I have an appointment with Sir Graham Forbes at four-thirty. I think it might be quite a good idea if you came along with us, Gerald.

GERALD: Yes. Yes, perhaps it would.

TEMPLE: Gerald, what time was it when you left the Savoy?

GERALD: Oh, about nine-thirty. (*Slightly puzzled*) Why do you ask?

TEMPLE: And you went straight to your office?

GERALD: Yes.

PRYCE enters.

TEMPLE: My hat and coat, Pryce.

PRYCE: Yes, sir.

Exit PRYCE.

TEMPLE: Was Ann annoyed with you for leaving the hotel so early?

GERALD: Well, not exactly … annoyed. But I must confess she wasn't too pleased about it. (*Irritatedly*) Damn it all, I didn't want to go to the office! Certainly not at that time of the night! But you know how I'm fixed … and I simply loathe taking proofs back to the flat. (*He finishes his drink and places the glass on the small table*)

PRYCE enters. He assists TEMPLE with his overcoat and then exits. TEMPLE and STEVE cross to the bookcase.

67

TEMPLE: (*Pressing the button for the lift*) Have you got your car here?

GERALD: Yes.

TEMPLE: (*Pulling on his gloves and speaking casually*) Well, in that case, you'd better follow me. Unless of course you'd like to leave your car and pick it up later?

GERALD: I think my best plan would be …

The panel bookcase swings open, and as it does so the body of ANN MITCHELL falls forward from the lift. A small dagger protrudes from beneath the velvet dress. PAUL TEMPLE springs forward and catches the inert form. STEVE screams … in horror and amazement. GERALD stares … bewildered … and strangely silent. From the hilt of the dagger, TEMPLE extracts a square piece of white cardboard. His face is grim and determined.

TEMPLE: (*Reading*) "The Front Page Men" … (*He looks across at STEVE*)

BLACKOUT
END OF SCENE 3

ACT TWO

SCENE FOUR

SCENE: The same as Scene 1, Act 1. The office of Sir Graham Forbes, Assistant Commissioner of Police, Scotland Yard.

It is almost six-thirty on the evening of the same day.

When the curtain rises, SIR GRAHAM FORBES is seated at his desk facing PAUL TEMPLE and CHIEF INSPECTOR REID.

FORBES: (*Thoughtfully*) You know, I can't quite make up my mind about Brightman. He told us that, acting on instructions he received from The Front Page Men, he deposited a suitcase containing eight thousand pounds in the cloakroom at The Regal Palace Hotel. Now, we know for a fact that he cashed …

TEMPLE: (*Interrupting FORBES*) Dr Brightman did not deposit the money in the cloakroom, for the very excellent reason that they won't let you deposit a suitcase in the cloakroom at The Regent Palace. They have a luggage deposit in Lord Street.

REID: M'm. Are you sure?

TEMPLE: (*Smiling*) Positive, Mac.

FORBES: Well, that seems to tie us down to the fact that Brightman must be mixed up in this business. (*Puzzled*) In which case, why the devil did he visit Scotland Yard and tell us a purely fictitious story?

TEMPLE: In my opinion Brightman visited Scotland Yard because he realised that, owing to his friendship with Sir Norman Blakeley, he was already under suspicion. By walking boldly into the lion's den, as it were, he was hoping – to a certain extent at any rate – to undermine that suspicion.

REID: Aye … that sounds feasible enough.

TEMPLE: I've also got a hunch that he was rather hoping to find something out about Mr Goldie; that's probably why he brought the old boy into the story about his daughter.

FORBES: (*Surprised*) But if Brightman is, as we suspect, at least a member of the organisation, then surely he must know all there is about Mr Goldie.

TEMPLE: (*Smiling*) Providing Goldie happens to be a member of the organisation too. But supposing he isn't?

REID: Well, if he isn't, it's quite feasible that Brightman might have thought he was a C.I.D. man. In which case, when he mentioned the old boy, he was probably trying to either take a rise out of us, or pump you, Sir Graham, concerning Goldie's real identity.

FORBES: By God, Mac, I'm not so sure that isn't nearer the truth!

REID: Then we get back to our original problem, sir. Who the devil is Goldie?

FORBES: M'm! (*Abruptly changing the subject*) I do wish Miss Trent would hurry up. (*He glances at his watch*) I've got Lord Farrington calling to see me at seven.

TEMPLE: (*Crossing to the window*) I'm rather worried about it, she said she'd be here by five.

REID: (*Thoughtfully*) You know, the thing that really puzzles me at the moment is this new development.

TEMPLE: Meaning Ann Mitchell?

REID: (*Nodding*) Yes. Now why in the world should they want to get rid of Ann Mitchell?

FORBES: Had you known her long, Temple?

TEMPLE: (*Turning*) Off and on for about five or six years. She was on the stage, you know, before she married Gerald.

FORBES: I know one thing. I feel damn sorry for Mitchell. The poor devil looked absolutely done in.

REID: You don't think Ann Mitchell was … Andrea Fortune?

TEMPLE: The author of The Front Page Men?

REID: Yes.

FORBES: No – Mrs Mitchell wasn't Andrea Fortune, Mac – I can assure you on that point.

REID: (*Faintly surprised*) Oh?

FORBES: The name 'Andrea Fortune' is a pseudonym – but the writer in question has got nothing whatever to do with the Front Page Men: the real Front Page Men, I mean.

REID: You sound pretty certain of your facts, Sir Graham, if I may be so bold as to say so.

FORBES: (*Smiling*) I am pretty certain, Mac. You see this morning I had rather an interesting letter on the subject.

TEMPLE: From Andrea Fortune, Sir Graham?

FORBES: Yes, Temple … from … Andrea Fortune.

The telephone rings on SIR GRAHAM's desk.

FORBES: (*Lifting the receiver: on the phone*) Hello? … Yes … (*A slight pause*) Hello? … Oh, it's you, Hunter! … What's that? (*Delighted*) Oh, good man! … Yes … Yes, bring him up straight away … No, don't bother about that … Yes, Reid's here … (*He replaces the receiver and turns towards REID*)

71

Hunter's back! He picked up Danny Muller in a
public house near the Haymarket, just over half
an hour ago!

REID: Well, I'm damned, and I've been over that district
with a toothcomb!

*SIR GRAHAM rises and brings the vacant chair facing his
desk down centre.*

TEMPLE turns from the window.

*The door back centre opens, and DANNY MULLER enters
followed by HUNTER.*

HUNTER: (*Pleasantly surprised*) Why, Temple, I didn't
know you were here!

TEMPLE: (*Smiling*) Hello, Hunter! (*Looking at DANNY*) So
you've got Danny Muller, eh?

HUNTER: Yes, after patronising practically every pub in
town. (*He smiles at REID*)

DANNY: (*Angry*) What the 'ell is the idea of dragging me
along 'ere? Anybody would think I was a blasted
tea-leaf!

FORBES: (*Quietly, pointing to the chair*) Sit down, Muller.

DANNY: Now just you listen to me! If you ruddy …

FORBES: (*Quietly*) Sit down!

There is a slight pause.

DANNY: (*Suddenly*) Ol'right … Ol'right, if that's what you
want.

*DANNY sits. SIR GRAHAM looks across at TEMPLE and
nods. TEMPLE leans against the desk, facing DANNY's
chair. He stares for a second or two before speaking. He is
nervous and apprehensive.*

TEMPLE: When did you last see Brightman, Danny?

DANNY: 'Ere, not so much of the Danny, I'm no pal of
yours!

TEMPLE: (*With a polite little bow*) Very well, Mr Muller,
when did you last see Brightman?

72

DANNY: I don't know who tha 'ell you're talking about.

TEMPLE: Don't you? I'm talking about the gentleman who happens to be sitting pretty. The gentleman who does not happen to be at Scotland Yard.

DANNY: (*Angrily*) I've got my rights the same as anyone else. I'm not going to sit 'ere listening to this ruddy nonsense!

TEMPLE: (*Quietly*) Aren't you, Danny?

DANNY: (*Still angry, but also rather frightened*) You've got nothing on me an' …. an' I've no right to be treated like this!

FORBES: You're under arrest, Muller, although apparently you don't seem to realise the fact.

DANNY: Under arrest! What the 'ell for?

There is a tiny pause.

TEMPLE: (*Softly*) For murder …

DANNY: (*Staggered*) Murder!

FORBES: Yes, Danny, the murder of Chubby Wilson.

DANNY: (*Frightened*) Chubby … Chubby Wilson …?

TEMPLE: That's right, Danny. (*Pleasantly*) Surely you remember Chubby Wilson, he was picked out of the river shortly …

DANNY: (*Desperately*) I never touched him! I swear to God, I never touched him!

TEMPLE: (*Crossing centre*) Then who did?

There is a pause.

DANNY: I don't know.

TEMPLE: (*Casually*) All right. All right, if that's how you feel about it. (*He turns towards SIR GRAHAM; he is deliberately casual*) I don't see that it makes a great deal of difference, Sir Graham. We know that Muller's mixed up with The Front Page Men, therefore he was partly responsible at any rate

73

for the murder of Superintendent Harvey, because it …

DANNY: (*Rising from his chair, indignantly*) That's a lie! That's a dirty lie!

TEMPLE: (*Turning*) Is it, Danny? (*Smiling*) How are you going to prove it?

DANNY: (*Sitting down again*) You think you're the clever one, don't you, Mr Temple!

TEMPLE: No. You're the clever one, Danny, if you use your head.

DANNY: (*Suspiciously*) What d'you mean?

TEMPLE: (*Softly*) Talk …

DANNY: I'm – I'm not a squealer! I'm not a blasted squealer!

HUNTER: Don't be a damn fool, Danny!

REID: You've got nothing to lose, man, don't you realise that?

DANNY: (*Vehemently*) Leave me alone! For God's sake leave me alone! (*He leans forward, his head in his hands*)

A slight pause.

FORBES: Danny … who are … The Front Page Men?

DANNY: I … I don't know!

TEMPLE: (*Reproachfully*) Danny …

DANNY MULLER slowly raises his head. He is obviously frightened.

REID: Well …?

DANNY: Brightman … Swan Williams … Lucky Gibson … a girl called Diana Fresnay … and … and Jimmy Mills　　　　…

FORBES: And the leader … Front Page Man, No 1 …?

DANNY stares first at HUNTER, then at REID, TEMPLE and SIR GRAHAM. He is strangely frightened and almost trembling with emotion.

74

HUNTER: (*Softly*) Well, Danny?

DANNY: I – I don't know. I don't know, I tell you!

DANNY once again buries his head in his hands. HUNTER takes a cigarette and thoughtfully taps it on the side of his case. SIR GRAHAM and TEMPLE are staring at DANNY. After a little while, DANNY raises his head. Not only is he trembling, but he appears on the verge of a mental breakdown.

DANNY: (*Weakly*) I'll – I'll talk … But first I … I want a drink … I must 'ave a drink!

FORBES: (*Gently*) Yes. Yes, all right, Danny. (*He turns towards his desk*)

TEMPLE: (*To SIR GRAHAM*) It's all right, Sir Graham. (*He takes the silver flask from his pocket, and pours a quantity of the liquid into the screw cup*) Here we are, Danny … (*He crosses to the chair*)

DANNY: Thanks. (*He takes the cup and swallows its contents in a single gulp*)

There is a tiny pause.

FORBES: (*Gently*) Now, Danny, you were going … (*He stops*)

They all stare at DANNY with astonishment as he rises from the chair, his face contorted with agonized bewilderment. He stumbles forward a little way, then collapses.

HUNTER: (*Amazed*) What the devil's the matter with him?

REID: Is the man out of his mind!

FORBES: What on earth …?

TEMPLE kneels down beside DANNY and feels his pulse. After a second or two he straightens himself.

TEMPLE: (*Quietly*) He's dead.

FORBES: Good God!

HUNTER: (*Staggered*) Dead …!

REID takes the flask cup from TEMPLE and looks across at him with obvious surprise.

FORBES: What is it, Mac?
REID: I should say the poor devil is dead! (*He offers SIR GRAHAM the cup*) There's enough cyanide in here to kill a regiment!
TEMPLE: (*Aghast*) Cyanide …
FORBES: My God, Temple, this is pretty serious …

The door opens and SERGEANT LEOPOLD enters.

FORBES: (*Annoyed*) What is it?
LEOPOLD: There's a gentleman to see you, sir. He said … (*He stares at DANNY with surprise*)
FORBES: (*Briskly, dismissing him*) I can't see anyone!!!!

SERGEANT LEOPOLD turns.

TEMPLE: (*Quietly*) Just a minute, Sergeant! Who is this man?
LEOPOLD: (*Turning towards TEMPLE*) It's a Mr Goldie, sir. A Mr J. P. Goldie.

CURTAIN
END OF ACT TWO

ACT THREE
SCENE ONE

SCENE: The same as Scene 4 Act 2. The office of Sir Graham Forbes, Assistant Commissioner of Police, Scotland Yard. Fifteen minutes later.

When the curtain rises, PAUL TEMPLE and SIR GRAHAM are the only occupants of the room. SIR GRAHAM is at the telephone on the large desk; TEMPLE is near the window. The chair, previously occupied by Danny, is now facing the desk.

FORBES: (*On the phone*) … Yes … M'm? … Are you sure, Bradley? … No. No, nothing like that … M'm? … Yes … Yes, all right … No, I should let Wade have a look at the flask … Oh, by the way … What the devil made you send Goldie to see me? … M'm? … No, not yet … Yes … Yes, all right, Bradley. (*He replaces the receiver*)

TEMPLE: Well?

FORBES: They've made a pretty thorough examination of the flask, but it doesn't seem to tell us a great deal.

TEMPLE: Are there any other fingerprints besides mine?

FORBES: There's a suggestion of one, but it seems very doubtful whether they'll be able to make anything out of it. (*He crosses in front of the desk*) You know, there's no doubt about it, Temple, that cyanide was meant for you. And by God, you'll have to watch your step! (*He turns and takes a cigarette from the desk*)

TEMPLE:	(*Offering a light from his lighter*) Frankly, I'm rather worried about Miss Trent, she should have been here hours ago.
FORBES:	I told Hunter to get in touch with the newspaper.
TEMPLE:	I wish to God I'd let you get that drink, Sir Graham, instead of offering Danny the flask.
FORBES:	It's perhaps a good job you didn't, Temple.
TEMPLE:	M'm – he'd have talked, I don't think there's any doubt about that.

SERGEANT LEOPOLD enters. He places several foolscap documents on the desk.

LEOPOLD:	(*Indicating the documents*) For the warrant cards, sir. Inspector Reid asked me to say that it was urgent.
FORBES:	Oh, yes. (*Return to the desk*) I suppose Mr Goldie's still waiting, Sergeant?
LEOPOLD:	Yes, sir.
FORBES:	(*Sitting at his desk*) All right, I'll see him now.
LEOPOLD:	Very good, sir.

EXIT SERGEANT LEOPOLD.

TEMPLE:	What made you send for Goldie?
FORBES:	(*Signing the documents*) I didn't send for him. This is entirely Bradley's doing. He asked Goldie to visit Scotland Yard and then suddenly took it into his head that I ought to have a word with the old boy. (*Slightly amused*) I rather fancy our learned Bradley found Mr J. P. Goldie somewhat of an enigma. (*He signs the rest of the documents*) You know, Temple, I'm rather worried about this old boy. There are certain people who are victims of what I suppose you might call

78

'Confidential circumstances'. I'm just wondering whether Goldie happens to be one of them.

TEMPLE: (*Quietly*) You think it was just a coincidence that Goldie happened to be at Sir Norman Blakeley's? Just a coincidence that he …

FORBES: (*Interrupting TEMPLE*) No … No … No; don't get the wrong impression, Temple. My personal opinion is that Goldie's mixed up in this business, on the other hand however one mustn't ignore the fact that it's quite likely that he isn't. Indeed, the only evidence which indicates that he is, is purely circumstantial.

TEMPLE: (*Smiling*) Don't forget a great many men have been convicted on circumstantial evidence.

SERGEANT LEOPOLD enters, followed by Mr GOLDIE.

LEOPOLD: Mr Goldie, sir.

Exit SERGEANT LEOPOLD.

FORBES: (*Pleasantly*) Good evening, Mr Goldie. (*Indicating the chair facing his desk*) Do sit down.

GOLDIE: Good evening, sir. (*Turning towards TEMPLE*) Why, hello, Mr Temple! This is indeed a pleasure.

TEMPLE: (*Shaking hands*) How are you, Mr Goldie?

GOLDIE: I called round to see you this afternoon, Mr Temple, but unfortunately you were out at the time.

TEMPLE: Yes, so my man told me. What was it you wanted to see me about?

GOLDIE: Oh, nothing really important. A client of mine happens to have a Bluthner for sale – a really beautiful model – I thought perhaps you might be interested. (*Apologetically*)

79

	Remember, you did mention something about changing your piano so I ...
TEMPLE:	Yes. Yes, of course. Perhaps you could get your client to drop me a note?
GOLDIE:	Yes. Yes, I'll do that with pleasure. (*He sits, and turns with a somewhat disarming smile towards SIR GRAHAM*)
FORBES:	I'm – I'm sorry to have kept you waiting.
GOLDIE:	Oh, that's quite all right.
FORBES:	I think you've already had a chat with Superintendent Bradley, but ...
GOLDIE:	(*Nodding*) Yes, sir.
FORBES:	But since there are one or two questions which I should rather like to ask you – er – personally, I thought ...
GOLDIE:	Well, if I can be of any assistance, Sir Graham.
FORBES:	I'm rather interested in a client of yours, Mr Goldie. A gentleman by the name of Brightman.
GOLDIE:	(*Puzzled*) Brightman? But surely that must be the same person that Superintendent Bradley mentioned?
FORBES:	Quite possibly.
GOLDIE:	I'm afraid he's not a client of mine, Sir Graham, I've already explained that to the Superintendent.
FORBES:	(*Quietly surprised*) Not a client of yours?
GOLDIE:	No, sir.
FORBES:	Is he a friend or ... an acquaintance?
GOLDIE:	(*Shaking his head*) To the best of my knowledge, sir, I've never even met the gentleman.

FORBES: I see. (*He takes a paper, and a rough press photograph from a folder on his desk*) Well, does this address mean anything to you, Mr Goldie? (*Reading from the paper*) Dr Brightman, Green Gables, Honeyford Avenue, Hampstead.

GOLDIE: No, sir.

FORBES: M'm. Then I can take it that you've never visited Dr Brightman's house, professionally or ... otherwise?

GOLDIE: Why, no, Sir Graham!

FORBES: (*Offering GOLDIE the photograph*) This is a photograph of Dr Brightman.

GOLDIE: (*Taking the photograph*) Thank you. (*He studies it*)

The buzzer sounds on the dictograph.

FORBES: (*Knocking down the switch*) Yes ...?

LEOPOLD: (*Off: from the dictograph*) Superintendent Wade would like to see you, sir.

FORBES: Is it urgent?

LEOPOLD: (*Off: from the dictograph*) Yes, sir.

FORBES: All right; tell the superintendent I'll be down straight away.

SIR GRAHAM moves the switch into position on the dictograph, then rises.

GOLDIE: (*Returning the photograph*) I've never seen this gentleman before, Sir Graham.

FORBES: (*Taking the photograph*) There's no doubt in your mind?

GOLDIE: (*After a tiny pause*) None whatever, sir.

FORBES: Thank you. (*Moving centre*) Will you excuse me, Mr Goldie? I rather want to have a word with a colleague of mine. I shan't keep you waiting above a couple of minutes.

81

GOLDIE: I'm in no hurry, sir.

FORBES: Oh, good. (*To TEMPLE*) Excuse me, Temple.

SIR GRAHAM crosses to the door.

TEMPLE: You might have another word with Hunter about Miss Trent, Sir Graham.

FORBES: (*Nodding*) Yes. Yes, I will.

Exit SIR GRAHAM.

MR GOLDIE slowly turns with an amused twinkle in his eye.

GOLDIE: It would have saved a great deal of time if Sir Graham had simply asked for my fingerprints instead of – er – making use of the photograph of Dr Brightman.

TEMPLE: (*Laughing*) You've been reading too many detective novels, Mr Goldie.

GOLDIE: (*Quietly*) Mr Temple ...

TEMPLE: Yes?

GOLDIE: Who is this Dr Brightman?

TEMPLE: Well ... we thought he was a client of yours.

GOLDIE: (*Slowly shaking his head*) No. No ... we've never met ... I'm sure of that. (*Thoughtfully*) Although his name seems vaguely familiar. Is he a friend of Sir Norman Blakeley's?

TEMPLE: An acquaintance, I believe.

GOLDIE: (*After a slight pause*) Mr Temple, forgive me, but I couldn't help over-hearing your remark to Sir Graham about Miss Trent. I trust that she is not in any trouble?

TEMPLE: Miss Trent is merely exercising a female prerogative by being two hours late.

GOLDIE: Miss Trent had an appointment to see you at five?

TEMPLE: Yes.

GOLDIE: Dear ... oh, dear!

TEMPLE: (*Conversationally*) What do you do with yourself on a night, Mr Goldie – I mean – when you're not   working?

GOLDIE: Oh, I – er – read a great deal, you know.

TEMPLE: Ah, yes! (*There is a tiny pause*) Tell me, have you read a novel called 'The Enchanted Meadow'?

There is a pause.

GOLDIE: No. No, I don't think so.

TEMPLE: It was originally a play. A very successful one too; I don't know whether you ever saw it or not?

GOLDIE: (*Quietly; facing TEMPLE with a steadfast gaze*) No. No ... I ... don't think I did, Mr Temple.

There is a long pause then SERGEANT LEOPOLD enters.

LEOPOLD: (*Addressing GOLDIE*) I beg your pardon, sir, but the Assistant Commissioner would like to see you in Inspector Hunter's office.

GOLDIE: (*Amused*) Good gracious me! (*He rises*) I seem to be making quite a circular tour of Scotland Yard. (*Holding out his hand*) Well, goodbye, Mr Temple ... No doubt we shall meet again.

TEMPLE: Goodbye, Mr Goldie. (*He shakes hands*)

GOLDIE cross to back centre, then slowly turns.

GOLDIE: Oh – er – what was that book called, Mr Temple, the one you mentioned?

TEMPLE: 'The Enchanted Meadow.'

GOLDIE: Ah, yes ... 'The Enchanted Meadow' ... Now I   come to think about it the title does seem vaguely familiar. (*He smiles*)

LEOPOLD: This way, sir.

Exit GOLDIE and SERGEANT LEOPOLD.

83

TEMPLE is faintly amused. Once again, and somewhat absent-mindedly, he crosses over to the window and stands looking down into the square below.

SIR GRAHAM enters from the office right, he is obviously worried, and stands for a moment or two watching TEMPLE.

FORBES: (*Softly*) Temple …

TEMPLE: (*Turning; surprised*) Hello, Sir Graham!

FORBES: (*Quietly*) I've been talking to Hunter.

TEMPLE: What is it? (*Apprehensively*) Sir Graham, what's the matter?

FORBES: A car called for Miss Trent nearly two hours ago
…   It was supposed to be from Scotland Yard.

TEMPLE: From Scotland Yard? (*Aghast*) My God, you mean … The Front Page Men …?

FORBES: (*Nodding*) Yes. (*Grimly*) Now, by God, whatever happens – we've got to find that warehouse!!!!

BLACKOUT
END OF SCENE ONE

ACT THREE
SCENE TWO

SCENE: The warehouse near Redhouse Wharf. The same as Act 2 Scene 2.

It is 9.15 the following evening.

When the curtain rises the stage is deserted. Suddenly, from the room above the warehouse, STEVE's voice can be heard calling for help. Her screams are quickly, and rather significantly, cut short. The telephone commences to ring. There is a pause.
DIANA enters from the right and crosses to the telephone. She lifts the receiver, and by means of a ring on her finger, taps a few bars of Morse code on the mouthpiece of the telephone. DIANA waits for the return signal, then speaks:

DIANA: Hello? ... No ... Not, not yet, Max! ... No, not even Brightman! ... (*Anxiously*) I'm worried; is everything all right? ... (*A tiny pause*) Yes ... she's here ... Oh, about the same ... (*Pause*) Max ... Are you sure everything is ... all right? ... Yes ... I'm listening ... Geneva? ... (*Quietly*) I see ... Well, take care, Max! ... Take care, for God's sake! ... All right, darling ... Goodbye! (*She replaces the receiver*)
The sound of a car is heard. The headlamp beams flash across the window, and the car draws to a standstill. DIANA crosses to the window. BRIGHTMAN enters from the right. He wears a heavy motoring coat, is obviously rather excited, and is carrying his bag.
DIANA: (*Quickly*) Is everything all right?

85

BRIGHTMAN:	Yes. We had a hell of a game with one of the cars.
DIANA:	Where's Jimmy and the others?
BRIGHTMAN:	They should be here soon.
DIANA:	The plan worked?
BRIGHTMAN:	(Nodding) Perfectly. (*Softly*) My God, you've never seen anything like this Nurembourg Collection. (*Crosses to the cocktail cabinet and places his bag on the floor*)
DIANA:	Has Jimmy got the stuff?
BRIGHTMAN:	Yes. (*Mixing a drink*) I say, what happened about that girl ... Steve Trent? Is she still at the flat?
DIANA:	No. She's here.
BRIGHTMAN:	(*Turning*) Here?
DIANA:	Yes.
BRIGHTMAN:	(*Frowning*) That's a bit stupid, isn't it?
DIANA:	Max daren't keep her at the flat any longer, she was getting out of hand.
BRIGHTMAN:	Did you have any trouble with her?
DIANA:	At first. We were nearly picked up in Oxford Street – she screamed like hell.
BRIGHTMAN:	M'm. (*He drinks*) Lucky was very good tonight, he worked like a trojan.
DIANA:	And Lord Romer ...?
BRIGHTMAN:	That was the easiest part of the whole business. The old boy never murmured.
DIANA:	(*Quietly*) I'm glad you arrived first, Andrew. I wanted to talk to you.
BRIGHTMAN:	Yes. I wanted to see you too ... that's why I came on ahead.
DIANA:	(*Slightly surprised*) Oh? What did you want to see me about?

There is a slight pause.

BRIGHTMAN: Can't you guess?

A long pause.

DIANA: Max has no intention of double-crossing you, if that's what you're thinking. You've been far too valuable. We respect both your intelligence and your courage. (*After a moment*) But the others, well …

BRIGHTMAN: What about the others?

DIANA: (*Watching BRIGHTMAN; softly*) They've got to go.

BRIGHTMAN: Why?

DIANA: You know perfectly well why … the Nurembourg job is the finish … the finish of The Front Page Men. In a very short while they'll have a warrant out for every one of us – excepting Lorraine.

BRIGHTMAN: Did … Muller talk?

DIANA: No. He's dead.

BRIGHTMAN: Dead!

DIANA: Yes. (*As she watches BRIGHTMAN, DIANA realises that he is turning over the position in his own mind*) Supposing they pick up Jimmy … or Lucky … or Swan for that matter. I shouldn't feel too happy about things, would you?

BRIGHTMAN: (*Quietly*) No. Lucky would talk … there's no doubt about that.

DIANA: They're dangerous, Andrew. This Nurembourg job has made them more dangerous than ever … they've got to go.

BRIGHTMAN: (*Thoughtfully*) Yes. Yes, perhaps you're right.

DIANA:	Max wants us to leave for Switzerland almost immediately. He'll join us later.
BRIGHTMAN:	Do the boys know about the Geneva hideout?
DIANA:	I'm afraid so. That's what makes them so dangerous.
BRIGHTMAN:	(*Indicating the room above*) What about the girl?
DIANA:	(*Quietly*) Max will take care of her … don't worry.
BRIGHTMAN:	(*Puzzled*) Diana, why did he bring her here? What's the point?
DIANA:	She's Richard Harvey's sister …
BRIGHTMAN:	(*Slowly*) I'm beginning to see daylight. (*Thoughtfully*) So Superintendent Harvey had a sister …? I didn't know that.
DIANA:	No. Neither did Max until Paul Temple kindly supplied the information.
BRIGHTMAN:	Temple? We've still got that little matter to attend to.
DIANA:	Don't worry about Temple. While we've got the girl, his hands are tied. (*Looking at her wristlet watch*) We haven't much time, Andrew.

BRIGHTMAN *takes off his overcoat and throws it across one of the chairs. He picks up his bag, crosses to the table, then opens it. He extracts a tiny bottle and by the light of the reading lamp scans the label.*

BRIGHTMAN:	Jimmy should be the first here. Swan and Lucky are coming together. (*He closes the bag*)
DIANA:	What are you going to …?
BRIGHTMAN:	(*With a smile*) You'll soon see. (*He crosses to the cocktail cabinet and mixes a whisky*

88

and soda. He brings this down to the table)
That's yours … now when Jimmy arrives be
drinking – at all costs he mustn't suspect
anything.

BRIGHTMAN returns to the cabinet and mixes a second drink which he places on the far side of the cabinet. He then takes the small bottle and empties its contents into the whisky decanter.

A car is heard approaching the warehouse. The beam from the headlamps crosses the window.

DIANA: (*At the window*) It's Lucky!

BRIGHTMAN: (*Surprised*) Isn't Jimmy with him?

The car stops.

There is a pause.

DIANA: (*Peering out of the window*) No.

BRIGHTMAN: He must be coming with Swan. (*He takes
his drink from the cabinet*) You know what
to do?

DIANA returns centre.

LUCKY enters from the right.

BRIGHTMAN: (*Pleasantly*) Hello, Lucky! I thought you
were coming with Swan?

LUCKY: (*Overwrought*) No. My God, we've 'ad a
time of it. They must have got the alarm out
pretty snappy. A rozzer stopped us just
outside of Guildford.

BRIGHTMAN: (*Quickly*) What happened?

LUCKY: Well …

BRIGHTMAN: (*Alarmed*) You didn't …?

LUCKY: Yes – I let him have it.

BRIGHTMAN: (*Angrily*) You blasted fool, Lucky, why …

LUCKY: It's all very well talking … we were in a
jam!

DIANA: (*Quietly*) Why did you change cars?

89

LUCKY: (*Crossing to the cocktail cabinet*) Swan was all shot to pieces, he couldn't drive. (*He takes the decanter and mixes a whisky and soda*) We – we had to get rid of him.

BRIGHTMAN: Get rid of him!

DIANA: (*Quickly*) What happened?

LUCKY: It's all right – he's taken care of. We dropped him in a backwater – it'll be twenty-four hours at least before he's picked up.

BRIGHTMAN: Is Jimmy all right?

LUCKY: Yes. (*He drinks*) This is the biggest job we've ever tackled, there's no doubt about that. (*He looks at   his glass*) What's the matter with this stuff? (*He drinks again*) Taste seems a bit funny, doc …

BRIGHTMAN: You've still got the jitters, Lucky!

BRIGHTMAN takes a good drink from his glass.

LUCKY: That rozzer was enough to give anybody the blinkin' jitters. (*He drinks*) There we … were.

LUCKY puts the glass down and leans against the cabinet.

DIANA: (*Quietly*) What's the matter, Lucky?

LUCKY: I … I feel dam' queer …

LUCKY rests his head in the palm of his right hand.

BRIGHTMAN: You'll be all right.

BRIGHTMAN crosses, removes the carpet, and lifts the trap door.

LUCKY: (*Dazed*) What … what are you doing?

BRIGHTMAN: (*Amicably*) I want you to give me a hand with the launch, Lucky. We want to have it ready, just in case …

LUCKY: Yes … all right. (*He moves away from the cabinet and immediately stumbles forward*) Doc … I feel …   dam' bad …

LUCKY moves towards the trap door and stands looking down.

DIANA: It's the excitement, Lucky …

LUCKY: (*After a pause*) The river's … fairly high … I didn't realise it … (*Feeling his heart*) … Doc … my heart's goin' like 'ell … (*Alarmed*) Doc … I'm all right … aren't I?

BRIGHTMAN: Yes! Yes, of course.

LUCKY moves on to the first step leading down to the river. BRIGHTMAN stands watching.

DIANA: (*Softly*) What about his car?

BRIGHTMAN: Drive it round to the back. We don't want Jimmy to see it.

DIANA: (*Nodding*) Yes, all right.

Exit DIANA.

BRIGHTMAN: Come on, Lucky! Come on!

BRIGHTMAN moves down the wooden staircase behind Lucky. LUCKY hesitates, as if in pain, his hand instinctively moves to his heart. He stumbles down several steps and is out of view, BRIGHTMAN stands watching for a second or two then he raises his foot and gives the unseen LUCKY a slight push. There is a desperate shriek as LUCKY hits the river. BRIGHTMAN straightens himself and returns to the room. He closes the trap door and is moving the carpet back into position when the sound of a car is heard.

DIANA enters from the right.

DIANA: Here's Jimmy!

BRIGHTMAN: (*Anxiously*) Did he see you moving the car?

DIANA: No. (*A tiny pause*) Is Lucky …?

BRIGHTMAN nods. JIMMY MILLS enters from the right. He is carrying a small black pouch.

91

JIMMY:	Hello, doc!
BRIGHTMAN:	Hello, Jimmy. Where's Lucky?
JIMMY:	(*Surprised*) Hasn't he arrived yet?
DIANA:	No. Why? Did he come on ahead or something?
JIMMY:	Sure.
BRIGHTMAN:	That's funny.
DIANA:	I thought he was coming with you, Jimmy?
JIMMY:	(*Crossing to the table*) Yes, we 'ad a spot o' bother an' changed over.
BRIGHTMAN:	What's happened to Swan?
JIMMY:	(*Nervously*) He – He … Well, if you must know – we 'ad to get rid of 'im. (*Quickly*) The bloody fool fell to pieces, doc, it was no use trying to …
BRIGHTMAN:	(*Softly*) That's all right, Jimmy. That's all right.
DIANA:	You did the wisest thing, we can't afford to take any chances, not at this stage!

JIMMY opens the pouch and exhibits the Nurembourg collection; a diamond necklace, two diamond pendants, an emerald ring, and a large sapphire brooch.

JIMMY:	Fair opens your eyes, doesn't it?
DIANA:	(*Softly; taking the emerald ring from the table*) Exquisite! Perfectly exquisite …
JIMMY:	You know, it's blinkin' funny Lucky isn't here because …

From the room above comes the sound of a chair overturning.

JIMMY:	(*Startled*) What's that?

JIMMY whips a revolver from his pocket.

JIMMY:	Who is it? Who's upstairs?
BRIGHTMAN:	(*Smiling*) There's no need to get excited, Jimmy. It's a girl called Steve Trent.
JIMMY:	Steve Trent …?

BRIGHTMAN: She's a reporter on The Evening Post.

JIMMY: A reporter! Well, you've certainly picked a ruddy good time to have a newspaper woman hanging around our necks!

DIANA: There's nothing to get alarmed about. We had orders from Lorraine to bring her down here, and ... and that's all we know.

BRIGHTMAN: What you need is a drink!

JIMMY: That's not a bad idea at that!

JIMMY crosses to the cocktail cabinet. He mixes a drink for himself from the decanter.

JIMMY: What's the Chief got in mind, Diana?

DIANA: What do you mean?

JIMMY: About this Trent girl ... This isn't exactly the time for slap an' tickle, if you ask me.

DIANA: No one's asking you, Jimmy!

JIMMY: All right! All right ... there's no need to fly off the 'andle!

JIMMY comes down centre with his drink. BRIGHTMAN takes his glass from the table.

BRIGHTMAN: (*Raising his glass*) Cheerio!

JIMMY: (*Absently*) Cheerio, doc.

JIMMY does not drink.

There is a slight pause.

BRIGHTMAN: What's the matter, Jimmy?

JIMMY: (*Thoughtfully*) I'm thinking about that rozzer; I hope to God Lucky did 'im in proper, he had a good decko at us.

BRIGHTMAN: (*Brightly*) You're nervy, Jimmy – what you want is a good stiff drink.

JIMMY: Perhaps you're right, doc.

JIMMY is about to drink then suddenly hesitates – his head cocked to one side.

BRIGHTMAN: What is it, Jimmy?

93

JIMMY:	I'm listening, that's all. Thought I 'eard voices.
DIANA:	(*Laughing*) You certainly are jumpy!
BRIGHTMAN:	For a man who's just made the best part of a cool three thousand you don't seem very bright, Jimmy.
JIMMY:	Three thousand?
BRIGHTMAN:	That's right. (*Indicating the Nurembourg Collection*) That's going to be your cut of the Nurembourg job, isn't it, Diana?
DIANA:	(*Nodding*) That's what Max said.
JIMMY:	(*Apparently delighted*) Three thousand smackers! Phew! That's what I call money!
BRIGHTMAN:	(*Brightly*) It's what we call money, Jimmy!
JIMMY:	(*Laughing*) Blimey, will I paint the town red!

They all laugh.

BRIGHTMAN:	(*Raising his glass*) Well, here's luck!
JIMMY:	Thank you, doc.
DIANA:	(*Pleasantly*) Drink up, Jimmy! (*She takes her glass from the table*)
JIMMY:	(*Thoughtfully*) Three thousand … Coo, fair takes your breath away, doesn't it, doc?
BRIGHTMAN:	(*Laughing*) It certainly seems to have taken your breath away. What the devil's the matter with you, Jimmy? Are you on the waggon?
JIMMY:	(*Puzzled*) On the waggon?
DIANA:	Yes … you're not drinking, Jimmy.
JIMMY:	Oh! On the waggon. (*Laughing*) Oh! Oh! Can you imagine it, doc! Me … on the waggon! Me … on the waggon! That's good! That's good!

They all laugh.

DIANA:	(*Amused*) Jimmy on the waggon – that's certainly funny!
JIMMY:	I was only on it once, doc, but I couldn't see straight.
DIANA:	(*Amused*) Well, cheerio! (*She drinks*)
BRIGHTMAN:	Cheerio, Diana! (*He drinks*)
DIANA:	(*To JIMMY*) Drink up, Jimmy!

There is a pause.

JIMMY stands watching. His right hand still holding his glass, his left significantly placed in his coat pocket.

BRIGHTMAN:	(*Quietly*) Why aren't you drinking?
JIMMY:	(*Taking command and moving across centre*) Because I'm not a bloody fool, doc!

JIMMY takes the revolver from his left pocket.

BRIGHTMAN:	(*Crossing towards DIANA*) Put that gun down, Jimmy!
JIMMY:	Stand still and keep those arms up … or by God I'll blow your blasted brains out!

BRIGHTMAN raises his arms.

DIANA:	Jimmy, don't be a …
JIMMY:	Shut up! (*Mimicking BRIGHTMAN*) Are you on the waggon, Jimmy? Drink up, Jimmy! Cheerio, Jimmy!

JIMMY starts chuckling, then suddenly stops, and holds out his glass towards BRIGHTMAN.

JIMMY:	'Ere, take this drink, doc … Take it!
BRIGHTMAN:	(*Recoiling*) No … no!
JIMMY:	(*Slowly*) What 'ave you done with Lucky?
DIANA:	I tell you we haven't seen Lucky!
JIMMY:	Don't tell blasted lies. His car's at the back!
BRIGHTMAN:	Now listen, Jimmy. If you take my tip …
JIMMY:	I'm taking nothing from you or anybody else, from now on, doc. I'm giving the

95

	orders, see! (*He thrusts the glass forward*) Now drink this!
BRIGHTMAN:	(*Alarmed*) No! No!
JIMMY:	Drink it!
DIANA:	(*Holding out her hand for the glass*) Here … I'll drink it.
JIMMY:	(*Turning; slightly surprised*) You …?
DIANA:	Yes. There's nothing in the glass except whisky. (*Pleasantly*) Come … I'll prove it.

There is a tiny pause.

JIMMY:	(*Suddenly*) All right! All right, Miss Clever! If that's how you feel about it. (*He offers her the glass*) 'Ere we are!
DIANA:	(*Taking the drink*) Thank you. (*To BRIGHTMAN*) Well, good luck, Andrew!

DIANA raises the glass and suddenly, with a flick of the wrist, throws its contents into JIMMY's face. He staggers back … blinded and bewildered.

JIMMY:	My face! My face! Oh, Gawd … my face! (*Turning to DIANA*) Why … you bitch, I'll …

BRIGHTMAN takes a small revolver from his inside pocket and, as JIMMY staggers forward, he strikes. JIMMY collapses.

BRIGHTMAN:	(*Smiling*) Smart girl!
DIANA:	Is he dead?
BRIGHTMAN:	(*Kneeling beside JIMMY and feeling his pulse*) No.

The red light appears above the cocktail cabinet.

DIANA:	(*Astonished*) Andrew … look! (*She points to the light*)
BRIGHTMAN:	(*Amazed*) Who the hell is this?
DIANA:	(*Puzzled*) I don't know.

The red light flickers. BRIGHTMAN rises, and suddenly crosses to the trap door. He stands listening.

BRIGHTMAN: (*Tensely*) Is it Lorraine?

DIANA: No. No, it can't be Max.

BRIGHTMAN: (*Crosses to the window and stares down into the courtyard*) I don't like the look of this, Diana!

DIANA: Is there anyone there?

BRIGHTMAN: No ... (*Peering through the window*) ... I don't think so.

BRIGHTMAN turns quickly and taking the Nurembourg Collection from the table and places it in his bag.

DIANA: What are you doing?

BRIGHTMAN: We've got to get out of here, and we've got to get out damn quick!

DIANA: But Max said he'd phone and if he finds that we've ...

BRIGHTMAN: (*Desperately*) For God's sake use your head, Diana!

DIANA: But what about the Trent girl?

BRIGHTMAN: To hell with the Trent girl! If we hadn't brought her back here this would never have happened! (*He closes the bag with a snap*) You can get in touch with Max when we get back to Town!

BRIGHTMAN crosses to JIMMY and commences a search of his pockets.

BRIGHTMAN: I'll join you in the car.

DIANA: Yes. Yes, all right.

EXIT DIANA.

As BRIGHTMAN finishes his search, the red light flickers; he rises, and crossing to the reading lamp, plunges the room into darkness. He then exits right after DIANA.

There is a pause.

The red light flickers once again, then remains steady. The trap door slowly opens and a thin beam of light, from a police torch, flashes across the room. CHIEF INSPECTOR REID enters, followed by SIR GRAHAM and SERGEANT DONOVAN.

REID: Can you find the light, Sergeant?

DONOVAN: (*Near the table*) Yes, here we are, sir! (*He presses the switch on the table lamp*)

REID crosses to the window.

FORBES: (*Staring at JIMMY*) Hello, look at this fellow!

DONOVAN: (*Crossing centre*) Jimmy Mills! M'm – he's going to be all right, too, by the look of things.

REID: (*Anxiously staring out of the window*) There doesn't appear to be any sign of Temple and party, sir.

FORBES: No. I didn't think they'd make it.

Suddenly STEVE enters from the right. She is tired and is obviously feeling the strain of the last twenty-four hours.

REID: (*Surprised*) Miss Trent!

FORBES: (*Coming forward*) Why, Miss Trent … are you all right?

STEVE: Yes. Yes, I'm all right now. I heard your voices and realised … (*She puts her hand to her head for a moment*) Mr Temple rescued me, he followed Brightman and the girl down to …

DONOVAN: (*Excitedly; pointing out of the window*) There's Mr Temple, sir!

From the courtyard the sound of a motor car engine is heard followed by a revolver shot.

FORBES: (*At the window*) That's Temple all right … and Bradley too, by Jove …

REID: (*Briskly*) Come along, Sergeant!

98

DONOVAN: Yes, sir.

Exit REID and DONOVAN.

FORBES: (*Slightly amused*) Temple seems to be taking the law into his own hands.

The car engine stops. A police whistle is heard followed by a second revolver shot.

STEVE: (*Swaying slightly with fatigue*) Is – Is he all right?

FORBES: (*Staring out of the window*) Don't worry about Temple, he can take care of himself. (*Turning*) But what about you, young lady, that's more to the point!

STEVE: (*Crossing to the settee*) I'm – I'm just a little tired, that's all. (*She sits on the settee*)

FORBES: I'll say you're tired!

FORBES crosses to JIMMY and kneeling down goes through his pockets. JIMMY stirs. He sits up.

JIMMY: (*Bewildered*) What happened?

FORBES: Feeling better?

JIMMY: Who – who the hell are you?

FORBES: (*Smiling*) Sir Graham Forbes, Assistant Commissioner of Police.

JIMMY: (*Stunned*) Good God! (*He staggers to his feet*)

SIR GRAHAM laughs. PAUL TEMPE enters from the right followed by REID and DONOVAN. TEMPLE looks slightly ruffled and is carrying an automatic pistol. He crosses to STEVE. DONOVAN takes charge of JIMMY.

TEMPLE: (*Anxiously*) Steve, are you all right?

STEVE: (*Smiling*) Yes.

REID: We've got Brightman and we've got the girl, in fact we've got all the swine, Sir Graham … except the one person that really matters … The Front Page Man.

TEMPLE: Yes, and we'll get him, Mac, too, before we're finished!

JIMMY: Well, you needn't think I'm going to do any talking, Mr Clever, because I'm not – see!

TEMPLE: (*Smiling*) Aren't you, Jimmy?

FORBES: (*To DONOVAN*) Take him down to the car!

DONOVAN: Yes, sir.

Exit DONOVAN and JIMMY.

REID: Miss Trent, how long had Brightman been here before we arrived?

STEVE: (*Thoughtfully*) Oh … about fifteen minutes, I should say. He arrived soon after the telephone call.

TEMPLE: (*Surprised*) The telephone call?

FORBES: Which telephone call do you mean?

STEVE: There was only one, Sir Graham. It was from Max Lorraine. I couldn't hear very well but I heard Diana say something about Geneva and then …

STEVE is interrupted by the ringing of the telephone. There is a tense pause. The telephone continues to ring. SIR GRAHAM crosses and lifts the receiver. He does not speak. After a second or two he replaces the receiver.

TEMPLE: What happened?

FORBES: They've rung off.

TEMPLE: Didn't you recognise the voice?

FORBES: (*Shaking his head, obviously puzzled*) No one spoke. I heard a kind of tapping noise, rather like Morse code, and then whoever it was replaced the receiver.

REID: What about tracing the call, sir?

FORBES: (*Lifting the receiver*) We can try. (*He dials the operator. TO TEMPLE*) I suppose that tapping noise was a signal and when I didn't

100

return it they ... (*Suddenly, on the phone*) Hello? Is that the exchange? Miss ... this is Sir Graham Forbes speaking, Assistant Commissioner of Police ... I've just received a telephone call and I want you to trace it for me ... M'm? ... Yes, I know all about that, Miss, but this is very urgent ... Yes ... Yes, just this minute ... M'm? ... Oh, this is (*He looks at the dial*) ... Kingston 9986 ... Yes, all right ...

There is a pause.

REID: Is she tracing it?

FORBES: I think so. (*On the phone*) Hello? ... Yes ... Yes, Miss? ... Mayfair 1742? ... One ... seven ... four ... two? Thank you, Miss? (*Replaces the receiver*)

STEVE: (*Bewildered*) Mayfair 1742? (*To TEMPLE*) But – But that can't be right?

REID: Why not? (*He follows her gaze to TEMPLE*)

FORBES: (*Puzzled*) Do you know the number, Temple?

TEMPLE: I ought to, Sir Graham. It happens to be mine.

FORBES: (*Amazed*) Yours ...?

REID: But what the devil is Lorraine doing at your place?

FORBES: Yes, and who is Max Lorraine?

TEMPLE: (*Grimly*) That's what we've got to find out!

TEMPLE crosses to the telephone, lifts the receiver, and dials. There is a pause.

TEMPLE: Hello? (*Another pause*) Hello ...? Hello, is that you, Pryce? ... Has anyone called this evening? ... I see ... is he there now? ... M'm? ... Just left ...? Oh ... Yes, I see ... How long did he stay? (*A slight pause*) M'm

...? No, that's all right. (*He replaces the receiver*)

FORBES: Well?

TEMPLE: There's only been one visitor to the flat this evening, and according to Pryce he's just left.

FORBES: (*Excitedly*) But – But who was it?

There is a pause.

TEMPLE: (*Quietly*) I'm afraid it was Hunter, Sir Graham, Inspector Hunter ...

SIR GRAHAM stares first at TEMPLE, then turns towards STEVE and REID. He is baffled and bewildered.

CURTAIN

END OF SCENE TWO

ACT THREE
SCENE THREE

SCENE: Same as Scene 3 Act 2. The lounge of Paul Temple's flat.

It is eight-thirty the following evening.

When the curtain rises the room is in darkness. The panel bookcase opens and reveals, in the dim blue light of the lift interior, the figure of PAUL TEMPLE. He enters, and from the switch near the panel, turns the lights on. As the panel closes, he crosses to the bay window and stands for a second or two staring down into the street. Suddenly, with a quick gesture, he draws the curtains. He crosses centre and as he does so, PRYCE enters from the right.

PRYCE: Good evening, sir!

TEMPLE: (*Removing his overcoat*) Hello, Pryce!

PRYCE: (*Helping TEMPLE with his coat*) Mr Goldie rang up about half past ten this morning, sir, but he left no message.

TEMPLE: (*Nodding*) That's all right, I've seen Mr Goldie.

PRYCE: Yes, sir. (*Turning; then suddenly hesitating*) Oh, I – I beg your pardon, sir.

TEMPLE: Yes?

PRYCE: (*Thoughtfully*) I've been thinking about last night again, sir. When Inspector Hunter arrived, I showed him straight into the library, and he was still in the library, sir, when I returned from the newsagents.

TEMPLE: That was just before I telephoned?

PRYCE: Yes, sir. But the library phone was disconnected, sir.

103

TEMPLE: (*Slightly amused*) But there was nothing to stop the Inspector from using the telephone in here while you were out.

PRYCE: No, sir. On the other hand, sir, it is possible that someone else might have entered the flat by means of the lift and …

TEMPLE: (*Laughing*) We'll make a detective out of you yet! (*A bell rings*) I rather fancy that's the bell, Pryce.

PRYCE: Yes, sir.

Exit PRYCE.

TEMPLE crosses to the cocktail cabinet and is mixing himself a drink when PRYCE re-enters.

PRYCE: Miss Trent has called to see you, sir.

TEMPLE is surprised; he replaces the glass on the cabinet and crosses centre.

TEMPLE: Miss Trent?

PRYCE: Yes, sir.

TEMPLE: (*Glancing at his wristlet watch*) Show her in, please, Pryce.

Exit PRYCE. He re-enters again followed by STEVE.

PRYCE: Miss Trent, sir.

Exit PRYCE.

STEVE: (*Smiling, somewhat nervously*) Hello!

TEMPLE: (*Anxiously; crossing towards STEVE*) Steve, you shouldn't have come here!

STEVE: It's all right, Paul, I've seen Sir Graham. (*With an affectionate pat*) He knows I'm here.

TEMPLE: (*Bewildered*) Yes, but Steve, what made you come?

There is a tiny pause.

STEVE: (*Quietly*) I came here tonight because … I think there's something you ought to know … something about me.

TEMPLE: (*Intensely*) My dear, don't you realise that at any moment now I'm expecting Lorraine … Max Lorraine. If once he …

STEVE: (*Interrupting PAUL*) Paul, you've got to listen to me!

A slight pause.

TEMPLE: Well?

STEVE: Two days ago, I wrote Sir Graham a letter. A letter explaining …

TEMPLE: (*Smiling*) Yes. Yes, I know.

STEVE: (*Bewildered*) You know …?

TEMPLE: (*Nodding*) Yes, my dear. (*Quietly*) I know that you are … Andrea Fortune.

STEVE: (*Relieved*) Oh, Paul, I've been so worried about it … so dreadfully worried. I've been intending to tell you about it for days now, but somehow or other I …

TEMPLE: (*Gently; taking STEVE by the arm, and leading her towards the bookcase*) I understand, Steve.

STEVE: Of course, I knew that the book had nothing whatsoever to do with the real Front Page Men, (*Puzzled*) except for the fact that for some reason or other they picked on the title as a sort of symbol.

TEMPLE: (*Faintly amused*) It's all right, darling.

STEVE: Then – Then you're not annoyed?

TEMPLE: (*Gently*) No, I'm not annoyed. (*Laughing*) But by Timothy, I hope you're not writing a sequel!

STEVE laughs, but she is interrupted by the ringing of the bell.

STEVE: Paul, that's …

TEMPLE: Yes!

TEMPLE turns towards the bookcase, but STEVE moves down stage.

STEVE: Paul ... I'm not leaving! (*She crosses to the recess*)

TEMPLE: What do you mean? (*Staggered*) My God, you can't stay here!

STEVE: Yes! Yes, I'm going to ... (*She moves towards the armchair*) I shan't make a sound ... he'll never suspect ... honestly, darling, I promise you!

TEMPLE: (*Shaking his head; yet hesitating*) No ... No, it's too risky, Steve!

PRYCE enters right, and as he does so STEVE slips into the armchair and is completely hidden from view. It is the same position for STEVE as in Act 1 Scene 2.

PRYCE: Chief-Inspector Reid to see you, sir.

TEMPLE hesitates; he turns towards the armchair, stands for a second or two undecided, then suddenly makes up his mind.

TEMPLE: Show him in, Pryce.

PRYCE: Very good, sir.

Exit PRYCE. TEMPLE glances across at the armchair. PRYCE re-enters.

PRYCE: Chief-Inspector Reid, sir.

REID enters right. Exit PRYCE. Temple crosses down centre.

TEMPLE: (*Anxiously*) Is anything the matter?

There is a slight pause.

REID: Yes. (*Quietly*) I'm sorry, Temple, but he's given us the slip.

TEMPLE: (*Staggered*) What! (*Softly*) Oh, my God ...

REID: According to Bradley, he entered the building over two hours ago.

TEMPLE: (*Surprised*) But wasn't Bradley supposed to be watching the place?

REID: Aye ...

TEMPLE: Then what on earth happened?

REID: I don't know. (*Bewildered*) I'm damned if I can make it out!

106

TEMPLE: Does Sir Graham know?

REID: Aye, an' he's like a cat on hot bricks! (*Obviously worried*) How many flats are there in this block?

TEMPLE: Oh, I should say about forty, and at least half of them must be unoccupied.

REID: T't – that make matters worse.

TEMPLE: But how the devil did he get in?

REID: It's difficult to say. Nelson seems to think by the Milford Street entrance.

TEMPLE: Milford Street? (*After a tiny pause*) There's an empty office on the ground floor, you know. It used to belong to the janitor.

REID: (*Surprised*) On the ground floor?

TEMPLE: Yes, and you can bet your bottom dollar he knew about it.

REID: (*Thoughtfully; quickly*) Rogers and Thornton are over on the other side – I'd better have a look at this myself.

REID takes a revolver from his pocket and slips back the safety catch.

REID: Where's the entrance to this office?

TEMPLE: It's near the side door. (*He crosses to the bookcase and presses the button*) I'll take you down.

REID: Oh, there's no necessity for that!

The panel opens.

TEMPLE: It won't take me a second.

TEMPLE and REID enter the lift. The panel closes.

PRYCE enters right followed by GERALD MITCHELL.

PRYCE: Mr Temple won't keep you waiting long, sir.

GERALD: (*Pleasantly*) That's all right.

Exit PRYCE.

GERALD takes out his cigarette case and lights a cigarette. There is a pause. He wanders across to the bookcase, then turns up left towards the recess and the armchair. As he approaches the armchair, the panel opens and TEMPLE re-enters. GERALD turns.

TEMPLE: Hello, Gerald! (*Pressing the button*) I'm sorry to have kept you waiting!

The panel closes.

GERALD: Oh, that's all right. I've only just arrived as a matter of fact.

TEMPLE: Good! (*He crosses to the cocktail cabinet*) You got my note?

GERALD: (*Smiling*) Naturally, that's why I'm here.

TEMPLE: Yes, of course! (*Taking the decanter*) What would you like to drink? Whisky and soda or …

GERALD: Yes, I think I'd rather like a whisky and soda.

TEMPLE: Splendid!

TEMPLE mixes the drinks.

GERALD returns centre and sits on the arm of the settee. TEMPLE crosses with the drinks.

GERALD: (*Taking the drink*) Thanks.

TEMPLE and GERALD both raise their glasses and drink. GERALD takes out his cigarette case.

GERALD: Cigarette?

TEMPLE: Oh, thanks. (*He crosses to the small table for the cigarette lighter*)

GERALD: How's the novel going?

TEMPLE: Oh – not too badly. I'm still finding the last chapter rather difficult.

GERALD: Is that what you wanted to see me about?

TEMPLE: (*Thoughtfully*) M'm? (*Suddenly*) Oh, no! I wanted to see you about something quite different.

TEMPLE places his glass on the table and takes the lighter.

GERALD: What … exactly …?

TEMPLE: (*He is looking at GERALD*) I wanted to see you about Ann.

GERALD: (*Surprised*) About Ann …?

108

TEMPLE: Yes. (*A slight pause*) You see … I happen to know who killed her.

GERALD: (*Rising*) Are – are you serious?

TEMPLE: Perfectly!

GERALD: But I've heard nothing about this from Sir Graham! Surely he would be the first to … (*Suddenly, intently*) Paul … Paul, who is the swine?

There is a long pause.

TEMPLE: (*Holding his gaze*) A man called Lorraine … Max Lorraine. (*He flicks the lighter*)

GERALD: Yes, but … who is Max Lorraine?

There is a second pause.

TEMPLE: You are … my dear Mitchell.

TEMPLE extinguishes the lighter and throws the cigarette on to the table. GERALD crosses down centre.

GERALD: Is this some kind of a joke? Because if it is, it's in damn bad taste!

TEMPLE: (*Shaking his head*) No. No, this isn't a joke. (*Softly*) My God, it isn't … (*He replaces the lighter*)

GERALD: (*Placing his right hand in the pocket of his jacket*) Why … why should I want to kill Ann …?

TEMPLE: (*Quietly*) For a very excellent reason, because she found out that you were Max Lorraine.

GERALD: (*With a little laugh*) Oh, Temple, for God's sake, man, don't be so silly!

TEMPLE: (*In the same quiet tone*) Because she found out about the Granville child and … 'The Enchanted Meadow.'

GERALD is surprised. He moves back several paces, in obvious consternation.

GERALD: What the hell are you talking about?

109

TEMPLE: I think you know what I'm talking about. (*He rises*) When Ann discovered that you were Max Lorraine, the poor girl was almost demented with anxiety ... and she made up her mind to tell me about it. (*He is looking straight at GERALD*) That's why she came to the flat that afternoon ... that's why you followed her here ... and why you attempted to cover yourself with a nonsensical story about ...

GERALD takes a revolver from his pocket.

GERALD: (*Unpleasantly*) You seem to have got things worked out very nicely, don't you?

TEMPLE: I think so. Although I must admit I've had a certain amount of luck on my side. I might, for instance, very easily have fallen for your trick with the gramophone record ... or the flask ... or (*Smiling*) the cigarettes ... (*Taking the cigarette box from the table*) I emptied the box this morning ...

GERALD: How did you know about the cigarettes?

TEMPLE: I didn't. But I knew that you must have had a reason for calling here last night. (*Casually*) That telephone call of yours was a mistake ... We traced it, I suppose you know that?

GERALD: (*Grimly*) Yes, you thought that was damned clever, didn't you?

TEMPLE: (*Evenly*) I thought so, yes.

STEVE rises from the armchair, and with her eyes glued on GERALD crosses towards the light switch near the panel.

GERALD: I don't often make mistakes, Temple, but I've an unpleasant feeling that I underrated your intelligence.

TEMPLE acknowledges the compliment with a polite little bow.

GERALD: I'm telling you this now because I've got a shrewd idea that it's about the last compliment you'll receive … from me … or anyone else. (*He raises the revolver*)

TEMPLE: (*Quietly*) I wouldn't do that, if I were you.

GERALD: No? (*Sarcastically*) If you're thinking of Sir Graham Forbes and his bright …

With a sudden start of suspicion, he turns towards the bookcase; at that precise moment, STEVE reaches the switch. The room is plunged into darkness. TEMPLE rushes forward and takes GERALD by surprise. A struggle ensues in which the table is overturned and the revolver falls.

TEMPLE: (*Calling to STEVE*) Get the curtains back, Steve!

STEVE dashes to the window and draws back the curtains. It is obviously a signal to the men below. As she returns centre, the panel bookcase slowly opens, the light from the interior of. the lift striking across the room. GERALD has thrown TEMPLE to one side, and he is picking up the revolver. He straightens himself and turns in complete astonishment towards the bookcase. The panel is now open – and revealed in the light of the lift – is the figure of Mr GOLDIE.

STEVE: (*Staggered*) Why … Mr Goldie!

GOLDIE: (*With the same wistful smile*) Good evening, Mr Temple. I told you that I should keep my appointment, didn't I?

GOLDIE is carrying a small automatic pistol; and he does not move from his position inside the lift.

GERALD: (*Nervously*) Who – who are you? What the devil do you want?

GOLDIE slowly turns his head in the direction of GERALD MITCHELL. He stares long and intently.

GOLDIE: It's a long story, Mr Mitchell, and I am just a little weary.

GERALD: (*Alarmed*) What – what do you mean?

111

GOLDIE: Do you remember Lester Granville … the actor …?

GERALD: (*Frightened*) Granville? My God, you don't mean that you're …

GOLDIE: His child was kidnapped … a little girl … he paid seven thousand pounds for her return … but she was not returned … (*Shaking his head*) … she was not returned.

GERALD: Don't stand there staring like … like …

GOLDIE raises his revolver.

GERALD: For God's sake, don't shoot! (*Terrified*) Don't shoot!!!!

GERALD suddenly realises that he has retrieved his own revolver from the floor, and he swings his arm forward; the moment he does so GOLDIE fires, GERALD sways slightly, clutching the back of the settee for support. The revolver falls to the ground. TEMPLE crosses towards him and is immediately followed by STEVE. The panel closes. TEMPLE hurries back centre, to the light switch. He switches the lights on, then returns centre. GERALD, although seriously wounded, is not yet unconscious.

SIR GRAHAM FORBES enters from the right followed by HUNTER and PRYCE.

PRYCE: Are you all right, sir?

TEMPLE: (*Supporting GERALD*) Yes. Yes, I'm all right. (*To FORBES*) Goldie shot Lorraine, Sir Graham! He came up by the lift!

FORBES: (*Breathless*) Don't I know it! Mac was on the entrance and Goldie laid the poor devil spark out!

TEMPLE: Is he hurt?

HUNTER: (*Amused*) No, not seriously.

GERALD stumbles forward; he is now almost unconscious.

STEVE: Paul!

FORBES: (*To HUNTER*) Get him down to the car, Hunter!

112

HUNTER: Yes, sir.

HUNTER and PRYCE take charge of GERALD. They exit right.

FORBES: (*Mopping his forehead with a handkerchief*) My God, what a night! I'm sorry about Goldie, Temple ... but we simply couldn't keep our eyes on him! (*Anxiously*) I hope to goodness he hasn't given Bradley the slip.

TEMPLE: Where is Bradley?

FORBES: He's on the Milford Street entrance. (*Replaces his handkerchief*) I'd better get down! (*He crosses right then hesitates*) Oh, and – er – many thanks, Temple ... for everything.

TEMPLE: (*Smiling*) You're welcome, Sir Graham!

Exit SIR GRAHAM.

STEVE: (*Slightly puzzled*) Paul, I rather gather that Goldie ... our Mr Goldie ... isn't really Mr Goldie at all?

TEMPLE: No, his name's Granville. Lester Granville. (*He sits on the arm of the settee*) For many years Lester Granville was a pretty successful character actor. He had one child; a little girl. About two years ago, the child was kidnapped, and Granville was instructed to pay seven thousand pounds for her release. He paid the ransom money but also, because he considered it his duty, he got in touch with Scotland Yard ... (*Softly*) The child was murdered.

STEVE: Oh, how horrible!

TEMPLE: The effect on Granville was really unbelievable. He left the stage and devoted his entire life to tracking down the person responsible for his daughter's death. And Granville was no fool, Steve! He knew what he was doing, all right. He realised that it was quite hopeless for him to try

113

and make a thorough investigation, unless he could first of all manage to conceal his real identity.

STEVE: And so he became Mr J. P. Goldie?

TEMPLE: (*Nodding*) And so he became Mr J. P. Goldie. Actually, Granville had known the real Mr Goldie for quite a little while.

STEVE: But what made Goldie ... our Mr Goldie ... suspect Gerald?

TEMPLE: It's rather a strange story. At the time when Granville's child disappeared, he was playing in a show called 'The Enchanted Meadow.' Ann Mitchell was also in the show, and she became quite friendly with his little girl. It was in fact through Ann that Gerald organised the kidnapping.

STEVE: (*Surprised*) Through Ann ...?

TEMPLE: Yes, but she was of course quite unaware of the fact. When the Front Page Men came into existence, Goldie suddenly realised that the novel – from which apparently the gang took their cognomen – was published by none other than Ann's husband – Gerald Mitchell!

STEVE: But I can't quite see why Gerald – or rather Max Lorraine – called his organisation the Front Page Men; surely by doing so he automatically drew attention to himself?

TEMPLE: Exactly! Which was really a brilliantly psychological move. The police knew that he was the publisher of the novel 'The Front Page Men' – and this put Gerald in a really excellent position! In the eyes of the law, he was merely the bright, but somewhat bewildered, young book publisher. Certainly, it automatically connected him with the case, but it also enabled the police to dismiss him as being an insignificant factor. The same move was made by Brightman. He deliberately brought himself to the notice of the police by saying that he had had his daughter kidnapped. Actually, this was a very carefully planned move on Brightman's part, for it enabled him to throw suspicion on Mr Goldie. (*He rises*) I saw Goldie this morning – or rather Granville – and he told me then the whole story about himself. (*Facing STEVE*) I don't think anyone will ever realise what that child meant to him, Steve. Before anything else in the world, he was determined to get even with Max Lorraine. When I sent for Mitchell, I knew perfectly well that Goldie would be ready for him. I told Sir Graham that at all costs Goldie must be stopped from entering the flat … (*After a slight pause*) But he wasn't, and I'm not so very sure that I'm sorry.

STEVE: But what's going to happen now? Do you think Goldie will escape from the police, or …

TEMPLE: I hope … I sincerely hope … that he won't try.

STEVE: But supposing he does … and succeeds?

TEMPLE: (*Quietly*) Then … bon voyage, Mr Goldie …

HUNTER enters from the right. He is rather exhausted.

STEVE: (*Anxiously*) What's happened …? Have you caught Mr Goldie?

HUNTER: (*Shaking his head*) No. No, he's given us the slip. God knows where he is! (*Pulling himself together*) I came back to tell you about Mitchell … or rather Lorraine … he's dead.

STEVE: Dead!

HUNTER: Yes, he died a few moments after we got him into the car. I thought perhaps you'd like to know.

115

(*With a sigh*) Well, personally, I can't say I'm sorry this business is over. It certainly put the wind up me.

TEMPLE: (*Puzzled*) Why do you say that?

HUNTER: (*Faintly amused*) As a matter of fact, Temple, I've literally been quivering in my shoes since the very first day I heard about Max Lorraine.

TEMPLE: But why?

HUNTER: Well, you see – apart from a distinct liking for Russian cigarettes – when I was a small and rather energetic youngster of about nine, I fell off a tricycle. It made a scar. A rather small scar above the right elbow.

TEMPLE: (*Amused*) Oh. Oh, I see.

STEVE laughs.

HUNTER: (*Nodding*) I daresay I shall see you both later.

Exit HUNTER followed by TEMPLE.

STEVE crosses to the recess and take her handbag and gloves from the armchair. She returns centre as TEMPLE re-enters.

STEVE: So Mr Goldie's … escaped?

TEMPLE: Yes, it looks very much like it … I'm afraid. (*He crosses to STEVE*)

STEVE: And you're sorry, Paul?

TEMPLE: (*Thoughtfully*) Not because he's escaped, Steve … no. Not because of what he did to Max Lorraine … but because I thought that, having had his revenge … having once achieved his main purpose in life … he would at any rate choose to stay behind … and face the music.

There is a slight pause.

STEVE: (*Suddenly*) Well, I want to get back to Fleet Street as quickly as possible. This story is rather important and the paper always …

TEMPLE: Steve …

STEVE: Yes?

TEMPLE: I – I was wondering if you … er …

STEVE: (*Smiling*) Well?

TEMPLE: If you'd … er … care to have dinner with me on … Thursday?

STEVE: Thursday? Yes, of course, I'd love to.

TEMPLE: Good, I shall be out – er – most of the day … so perhaps we can – er – lunch together, too?

STEVE: Yes, why not?

TEMPLE: We might even manage to have tea together as a sort of … er … sort of … er … er …

STEVE: (*Inwardly amused*) I'd love to.

TEMPLE: Oh … er … splendid. Well, that's about all … (*As an afterthought*) Of course, there is breakfast, but …

STEVE: I always have breakfast in bed.

TEMPLE: In bed?

STEVE: Yes.

TEMPLE: Oh, er … well, that's a bit awkward.

STEVE: (*Calmly*) Of course … we could get married.

TEMPLE: (*Without thinking*) Yes, I suppose we … (*Suddenly amazed*) What! I say … I say, are you proposing?

STEVE: (*Imitating TEMPLE*) By Timothy, Mr Temple! What do you think? (*Laughing*) What do you think?

TEMPLE: Well, of all the unconventional little devils!

TEMPLE takes STEVE in his arms, and they embrace. Suddenly, TEMPLE gives a start of surprise; he holds STEVE quite still.

STEVE: What is it?

TEMPLE: Listen!

There is a pause.

From the adjoining room can be heard the sound of a piano. It is being played softly, and with almost a strange charm.

PRYCE enters.

TEMPLE: (*After a slight pause*) Pryce, is that someone in the library?

PRYCE: Yes, sir. It's Mr Goldie, sir. Mr J. P. Goldie.

The piano continues.

CURTAIN
END OF THE PLAY

The Press Pack

… press cuttings about *Send For Paul Temple* – the stage play

Paul Temple on the Stage

Paul Temple, the radio detective, who appears in the flesh at the Alexandra Theatre this week, has achieved fame throughout the English-speaking world since he first starred in the Midland Region radio thriller series, "*Send for Paul Temple*" in 1938 – the work, by the way, of a Birmingham author, Francis Durbridge. The plays were heard by millions both in this country and abroad and created a BBC fan mail record.

Paul Temple gained particular support in Holland, and Dutch translations of the various Paul Temple plays – and the novel – sold well in that country. The detective became No 1 radio favourite with Dutch listeners. The character was called Paul Vlaanderen in that country, and his exploits were broadcast at a peak listening hour every Sunday evening. "*Paul Vlaaderen En Het Z4 Mysterie*" was being broadcast at the time of the Nazi invasion of Holland.

This Week's Shows

Armchair fans of Paul Temple, the radio detective, will enjoy Paul Temple, stage detective, in the Francis Durbridge thriller, "*Send For Paul Temple*" at the Alexandra this week. Every conceivable method of killing off the sleuth is tried, unavailingly, of course; the attempts merely leading Mr Temple on to greater glories in the detecting line.

Robert Ginns is very convincing as Paul Temple, and is ably supported by the indispensable woman journalist, Angela Wyndham-Lewis. The uniformed minions ever revolving round the modern detective of fiction are excellently led by

Denis Goacher as Chief-Inspector Reid, and another outstanding performance comes from Vernon Fortescue as Sir Graham Forbes.

Radio Thriller To Be Staged
Transition of plays and players, as well as features and frolics, from wireless studio to theatre, becomes more and more a matter of course, and the radio is fast becoming a trailer to the stage. The exciting BBC serial "*Send For Paul Temple*" will be familiar to many listeners, a large number of whom, no doubt will be only too anxious to see how Francis Durbridge's radio detective shapes behind the footlights.

The part will be played at the Alexandra Theatre next week by Robert Ginns, and with his girlfriend Steve Trent (Angela Wyndham-Lewis) Paul will figure in a new adventure on the old lines. Members of the Alexandra Repertory Company, reinforced by certain guest players, will excitingly adjust the hazards of crime and detection according to the author's formula. This play is scheduled for the usual fortnight's run.

Midlander's Radio Play Staged
One of the most successful of radio thrillers, "*Send For Paul Temple*," will have what I believe is its first stage performance in the city of its author, Francis Durbridge, who is a native of Birmingham when the Alexandra Repertory Company present it at the Alexandra Theatre next week. Robert Ginns will play the famous sleuth and Angela Wyndham-Lewis will play "Steve."

Paul Temple at the Alexandra
There are strange goings-on this week at the Alexandra where Paul Temple, the detective who has made a reputation on the radio is in session. To provide incident for this exciting sitting

it seems that the Newgate Calendar has been combed for material. A couple of kidnappings head the list and lead on to sterner stuff in the form of poisonings, shooting and dope dealings. Bodies fall out of lifts; screams rend the night; an innocent-looking gramophone spits forth bullets; and cyanide finds its way into harmless brandy flasks.

Francis Durbridge, the author, has thought of pretty much everything that is looked or listened for in the thriller; and, although the motives for all these misdemeanours are mixed to the point of obscurity, largess in the form of clues is broadcast, and we are kept too busy trying to distinguish between the authentic scent and the liberally-strewn red herrings to bother over-much about motives.

Of course, this nefarious exercise is the work of a gang: nothing less than a clutch of criminals is worthy of Mr Temple's monumental mind. Yet in the final scenes the case resolves itself into a chase with the mysterious leader. Your Jimmy, your Danny and your Lucky are more hewers of wood and drawers of water. Only in the last five minutes is the great man disclosed in all his splendid infamy; and strongly as we have suspected A and B, it turns out to be X after all. We did examine him during the first act, but dismissed him as not worthwhile, especially as A and B were more seemingly innocent. The game of spot-the-killer is often won by watching the least likely person on stage; but Mr Temple apparently must have a man worthier of his mettle.

The Alexandra Company takes to crime efficiently, not to say enthusiastically; and last night the legal traffic flowed quite smoothly except when the most important pistol of all roused titters instead of terror by faintly clicking when it should have cracked. Even this did not disturb the suavity and ease of Robert Ginns's likeable Paul Temple or the calm confidence of Vernon Fortescue and Denis Goacher as the men from Scotland Yard. Angela Wyndham-Lewis is the discreetly intelligent woman journalist indispensable to the modern detective; and Andrew Buck as Dr Brightman is the perverted practitioner indispensable to the modern crime.

Next Production: "Send For Paul Temple"

To hundreds and thousands of people all over the English-speaking world, this title will recall many an exciting half hour spent listening on the radio to Francis Durbridge's famous crime serials. Next week (by arrangement with Emile Littler) you will have the first opportunity to become acquainted with radio's most popular detective and his girlfriend "Steve Trent" in the persons of Robert Ginns and Angela Wyndham-Lewis. The novelist-sleuth and the dashing journalist will be involved in an entirely new adventure, an adventure even more exciting than any of their previous ones. Partly on the side of law and order and partly amongst the criminal underworld will be found all of the members of the Alexandra Repertory Company, together with several guest-artistes.

Alexandra Theatre Programme

Radio Detective Lives in Alex Thriller

However much you were thrilled by the exploits of Paul Temple, in those exciting half hours of fireside listening, that the odds are that in the flesh – he is at the Alexandra – you will think him a far better detective for the intimacy of a different technique, and the problem he sets out to solve will be the very problem that will keep you glued to your seat until the final curtain.

In his latest adventure there are as many thrills, and quite as much suspense as is good for the average individual. But the point that matters most is that it is all very good entertainment, and the Alexandra Repertory Company rise to its dramatic possibilities with spirit and vigour.

Robert Ginns makes Paul the real debonair character of a fictional detective, polished and elegant in all he does, and Angela Wyndham-Lewis plays Steve Trent, the dashing journalist, with power and conviction. In short, Francis Durbridge, the Birmingham author of the Paul Temple series, should be quite satisfied with the way in which the whole company makes his characters live.

Printed in Great Britain
by Amazon

77449862R00083